**Books are to be returned on or
before the last date below**

My life behind the scenes at...

Heart Magazine

Boys,
blues &
shoes

Cindy Jefferies

USBORNE

For boy band fans everywhere

First published in 2011 by Usborne Publishing Ltd., Usborne House,
83-85 Saffron Hill, London EC1N 8RT, England.
www.usborne.com

A CIP catalogue record for this book is available from the British Library.

JFM MJJASOND/11 02346/1 ISBN 9781409520214
Printed in Reading, Berkshire, UK.

Exciting news

Ellie squeezed through the crush of people on the bus. It had been standing room only since the last stop and she needed to get off in a minute. "'Scuse me. Excuse me." The bus was jerking along, as if it was pretending to be a kangaroo. Trying to avoid falling into an elderly woman's lap, she grabbed at a handle and realized she'd avoided the woman only to have trodden on a man's foot. "Sorry!" She wanted to giggle when the man looked through her without replying.

At last, the bus came to a sudden halt, and everyone standing up swayed in unison as they hung on. Ellie jumped off the bus as soon as the doors opened, stumbled, and almost fell. A passer-by put out a hand to help her but she didn't need it. "It's okay, thanks. My fault!" She hurried along the street, eager to get to her destination. In a very few minutes she was there. The huge glass-and-steel building always impressed her, with its double doors and huge lobby. This was where *Heart* magazine had its offices.

Ellie couldn't *wait* to get back to work in the Editorial Department. It seemed *ages* since she'd been here for her work experience. Since then, she'd been working hard at school, but – thank goodness – at last it was the Easter holidays, and now nothing could keep her away.

Heart was her friends' favourite magazine, and Ellie's too. It had all the best articles, great fashion pics, fun quizzes, and interviews with the celebrities they loved the most. Working for *Heart* really was Ellie's dream job, and she was so lucky that Angel Makepiece, the scary Editor in Chief, had said that she could come in during the school holidays.

Ellie had always wanted to be a journalist like her father had been, and she had always hoped to work for *Heart* when she was grown up. But she had never thought it would really happen. After all, *everyone* longed to work for *Heart*. Thanks to her Uncle Patrick, who was on the board of the magazine, Ellie had got work experience here last term. But after that it had been up to Ellie. She had been determined to show what she could do, and had so impressed Angel that she had been invited back. How cool was that!

Ellie paused outside the tall building. She was going to spend as much of the holiday as possible at the magazine. But she was under no illusions. She might have been invited back, but she knew she would have to prove her worth over and over again. There was no room for passengers at *Heart* magazine. But this was what Ellie thrived on. She was ambitious, and very determined to become a brilliant journalist. So it was hardly surprising she was feeling so upbeat. Ellie Ixos was on her way, and she really did have the holiday job to *die* for!

Ellie didn't mind how tough the Editor in Chief could be, or how exacting Francesca Mosse, her deputy, was. She was there to learn. It was a pity that Piano, the Editor's PA, had tried to treat her as the lowest of the low, but during her work experience, Ellie had made good friends with Sophie, the post girl, and Flynn, Sophie's gorgeous boyfriend, who worked in the IT Department. In spite of the ups and downs, it was the chance of a lifetime to gain experience here, and just arriving at the office made Ellie feel as if she was in *heaven*.

A shiver of excitement ran up her spine as she pushed open the heavy glass door. At reception she gave her name and got her pass.

Then, feeling very sophisticated, she headed for the lift. *Heart* was located on the third floor, where the magazine had its own reception desk just inside the large, open-plan office. Ellie got out of the lift, and went to the shoe cupboard in the lobby to change out of her boots. Everyone had to keep a pair of suitable office shoes at work, as Angel was very particular about her white office carpet, although Ellie had noticed that Angel didn't seem to mind when Ferdinand, her little dog, left hairs all over it.

Ellie pulled on her office shoes and hurried into the editorial office, wondering what the new receptionist would be like. The last one had been dismissed for her attempts to sabotage the magazine when she felt her potential had been overlooked. To Ellie's surprise, Piano Arnley-Armitage, the Editor's PA, was on reception, and looking thoroughly grumpy.

"Hi there, Pea-Are-No!" said Ellie, pronouncing the name in the way that Piano preferred.

"Oh, it's you," said Piano sourly, hardly glancing up.

"Where's the new receptionist?" asked Ellie, who could see that Piano's moods hadn't improved since Ellie had last been here.

"What new receptionist?" said Piano, sounding furious. "The one we took on when Carlotta was sacked left after a couple of weeks, and the temp agency sends us total losers. Being understaffed is *awful*. Another one is coming tomorrow, but goodness knows what *she'll* be like."

"Well, I'm here now," said Ellie, feeling sure that there would be lots for her to do. "And I can come in most days of the holidays."

Piano rolled her eyes. "Oh yes," she said. "I'm sure we'll all be very grateful for *your* expert help." She started to type furiously, as if Ellie didn't exist.

Ellie sighed, but she was feeling much too happy just being here to let Piano get to her.

"Do you know where my laptop is?" she asked, seeing no sign of it at the far end of the reception desk, where she had worked before.

Piano glanced up from her screen, looking even more annoyed than before. "You're not sitting here," she snapped. "I'm not having you cluttering up the reception area like last time, and I haven't got time to chat like Carlotta did. I've come over here so I can do two jobs instead of one." She paused. "Francesca said she'd sort out a small desk for you, but she hasn't had a chance to do it yet. You'd better use my desk for now." She pointed one dark-blue painted nail, and Ellie looked. She really was pointing at her own desk. Ellie's heart skipped a beat. How brilliant!

"Thanks," she said, giving Piano a wide smile. Ellie walked past Piano, and on into the large, open-plan office. Francesca Mosse, the Deputy Editor, was busy at her desk, looking as elegant as usual, but with a rather harassed expression on her face.

Ellie tucked her bag neatly under the chair at Piano's desk and logged onto the laptop that was waiting for her. It was wonderful having her very own desk, even if it was borrowed. It made her feel much more professional, and as if she really belonged.

On her screen, Ellie could see some of the articles that were going to appear in the next issue of *Heart*. She didn't want to read them all the way through just now, but it was great to have a sneak preview of what the next magazine would contain. It looked as if there was going to be a feature on swimwear. Ellie made a note to let her best friend Hannah know, because she'd been saying that she needed to go shopping for a swimsuit. There was also a little piece about the coolest colours for toenails.

"Hello, Ellie. How are you?" Francesca had finished what she was doing, and pushed back her chair, crossing one slender leg over the other.

"Fine, thanks," said Ellie. "It's fantastic to be back!"

"Well I'm afraid you're going to be kept pretty busy," said Francesca. "And as Piano has no doubt told you, we've had no receptionist again for a couple of days, which hasn't helped."

"That's okay," said Ellie. "I'll do whatever I can. What's happening this week?"

"Well…" Francesca looked resigned. "Angel has loads of meetings, so she'll be in and out a lot. We've got a boy band coming in tomorrow, which is a great opportunity for a feature, so we jumped at it when their PR people contacted us. They've got a new album coming out, and want to promote it. Oh, and someone has to go and collect some shoes from Jacob Frou. Joe is going to photograph the new collection for us, and Angel decided that the band members ought to be in some of the shots too. We need to make sure everything is in place at the right time. We don't want any hitches." She made a note on her pad. "The band has agreed, but I mustn't forget to confirm the models."

"Which band is it?" asked Ellie, hoping it might be one she liked. Meeting famous people wasn't the reason that Ellie wanted to be a journalist, but it was brilliant fun when she did – last time she was here she had met famous pop stars Pop and Lolly Lowther! She didn't want to waste any opportunities that might come her way.

"It's Zone One," said Francesca. She picked up on Ellie's expression and smiled. "So you're one of their fans too, are you?"

Ellie nodded. "They're fantastic!" she said excitedly. "Especially Al. He's the one with blond hair. He's my favourite singer *ever*."

Francesca laughed. "Well, it's nice to know that we're getting the right celebrities in for our readers *and* staff. Piano thinks they're great as well."

"Really?" Ellie hoped Al wasn't Piano's favourite too. Al was *hers*!

Francesca had stopped laughing and was looking more serious now. Ellie tried to suppress the bubble of excitement that was threatening to make her giggle, but it wasn't easy. The thought of actually seeing, and maybe even talking to Al from Zone One made it hard to concentrate on the Deputy Editor.

"You might not get much chance to hang out with them," Francesca was warning. "Your best opportunity will be when they arrive in the office at midday, before Angel takes them out to lunch. After that, of course, they'll be involved with the photo shoot, which will take a while. Once they're done they may be dashing off somewhere else, so it could be difficult to speak to them then. I will make sure you and Piano have a chance to say hello when they first arrive though."

Ellie beamed. "That's brilliant, Francesca. Just being in the same *room* as them will be amazing, and actually saying hello to the boys from Zone One...especially Al...will be *fabulous*. This is the chance of a lifetime for me. Wow! I'm actually going to be able to say hi to Al. I really can't *believe* it!"

"Okay!" said Francesca with a tolerant smile. "I get the picture. You're rather pleased to be working here again. Yes?"

"Yes!" Ellie knew her friend Hannah would be *green* with envy once she found out about the band. She loved them too, especially Jay, who tended to be their spokesman. But Ellie didn't want to give the impression that she'd be empty-headed from now until after she'd met the band. "If you have jobs for me to do I'd better get on with them," she said eagerly.

Francesca looked at her with approval. "You need to go and see Angel," she told Ellie before turning back to her screen. "Since the agency sent us so many unsuitable people she's decided to look over any new person herself when they come into the office to work, and even though you've been in before, she asked for you." She smiled. "I expect she wants to make sure all the staff are presentable."

Ellie immediately smoothed her skirt and hoped that her hair and make-up were okay.

"Don't worry," said Francesca, scrolling down a page on her screen. "You're fine. But hurry up. She'll be wondering where you are. I know she had a load of jobs lined up for Piano before we discovered that the agency was letting us down again. No doubt she'll want to give some of them to you."

Angel was notorious for making huge demands on everyone in the office, and Ellie had spent most of the time trying to avoid her when she was last at *Heart*. Since getting Angel's letter offering her holiday work, though, Ellie had felt a lot more confident. She took a deep breath. This was what working for *Heart* was all about. On her work placement here, she had been allowed to write a piece about Pop and Lolly, which had actually appeared in the magazine. Remembering that, she felt fired up, full of energy and enthusiasm. Yes, there were tight deadlines, and lots of stress, but there were also huge rewards. It had been a big thrill to get her article about Pop and Lolly published, and tomorrow she was going to meet Zone One!

2
Angel's list

Ellie went over to the door that led to Angel Makepiece's office. She knocked, and Angel's voice sounded through the door.

"Ye-es?"

Angel's usual voice was gentle and unthreatening. But this soft voice, cloud of blonde hair, and angelic, pink and white complexion were very misleading to the casual observer. Just as a pretty kitten has hidden, needle-sharp claws, so behind Angel's attractive exterior lurked an exceedingly bright intellect and a *very* sharp tongue.

Ellie opened the door and went in. Angel was sitting behind her desk, with Ferdinand's basket next to her. The tiny dog looked dreadfully bored, but began to wag his tail as soon as he saw Ellie. He seemed to be pleased to see her, which was nice. Although Ellie liked dogs, as far as she was concerned Ferdinand was a bit of a nuisance, because she'd often had to take him out for walks when she'd much rather have been in the office, learning about how to produce the magazine. But that was hardly his fault, so when Ferdinand got up and began to get out of his basket, Ellie was all ready to make a fuss of him.

Angel put her hand down to restrain the dog. "Not yet," she said. "Ellie will take you out later." He subsided onto his cushion again and Ellie looked at him. *That* was probably the reason he seemed to like her. He'd remembered that when she turned up he would get a lot more walks!

"Ah, Ellie..."

Ellie didn't believe the kindly tone of Angel's

voice one bit, and she hurried to show her gratitude for the job. "Thank you so much for writing, and offering me some holiday work. I'm thrilled to be back, and I can't wait to help out." She paused. "Francesca said you had a couple of jobs for me."

"One or two. I've emailed them to you. Piano will be very grateful. She's been getting a bit behind with having to man the reception desk so much. The jobs shouldn't take you too long." She gave Ellie a sharp look, taking in her hair, make-up, dress and shoes. After a long moment she nodded. "You look satisfactory. Off you go." She closed a drawer in her desk and began tapping the keys on her computer, taking care not to chip the dark pink nail varnish on her perfectly manicured hands. Ellie knew she had been thoroughly dismissed.

She backed out of the office, glad she'd got through the brief exchange so easily. The few minutes in the Editor's office had gone better than she'd feared. At least with a list of jobs to work from she'd be able to go through it logically, without waiting around to be given the next thing to do. She closed Angel's door quietly, as the Editor liked.

In spite of her determination to be sensible about the band, she couldn't stop thinking about Zone One, and especially about Al, her favourite. Would he really be as nice as he seemed in magazines and on the telly? She would simply *die* if Piano monopolized him and she didn't get a chance to say hello.

She drifted back to her desk in a dream, and opened the email from Angel. It did seem to be a very long list of jobs to do. But once she had studied it for a couple of minutes, Ellie was sure she'd be able to work out the most efficient way to get them all done. She needed her notebook, so reached for her bag.

She pulled out an old, black notebook that had belonged to her father. He had been a war correspondent, and had died before she had been born, so it was especially lovely to have, as he'd written comments in it that often seemed to speak directly to her. Today, when she opened it, her eye was immediately drawn to a sentence that she hadn't noticed before. *Experience everything life has to offer.* Well that, like most of his comments, was sound advice, and Ellie decided to do just that. Most of her jobs today seemed to be errands that needed doing out of the office. She'd be going to parts of the city she'd never visited before, and meeting new people. It was a perfect day to relish new experiences.

Ellie knew that lots of people were stuck in offices all the time, while she was getting to go out and about on errands. She might not get to write much today, but she was sure she'd have fun...and tomorrow she'd meet Al!

Ellie wiped the smile of anticipation off her face, and sternly told herself to concentrate on the list. She couldn't dream the day away, or she'd make mistakes, and get into terrible trouble. However gorgeous Al was, she simply must put him to the back of her mind. Daydreaming wasn't the way to experience everything life has to offer! She wrenched her mind away from boy bands and focused on the list on her screen.

Things like Angel's dry-cleaning were simple, because the shop was within easy walking distance of *Heart's* office, but collecting shoes for the photo shoot was bound to be a priority, and she had no idea where the shoe designer's was. It was almost certain to be a bus or taxi ride away, and that could take *ages* in heavy traffic. She'd need to ask advice about that.

As she pondered, Francesca paused in what she was doing and looked over to Ellie. "One thing, Ellie," she said. "Could you hurry down to the basement straight away, and collect the post?" Ellie was surprised. When she'd been here before, Sophie the post girl had brought it up. Ellie wondered why that had changed, but it would be good to see Sophie again. She was the nicest person in the office building, and Ellie couldn't wait to say a quick hello to her.

Ellie nipped down to the basement. The post room was by far the scruffiest place in the building, with worn paintwork, and scratched furniture. Sophie was there, busy emptying a large sack of post onto a battered wooden table.

"Ellie! I didn't know you were coming in today. Is it the holidays already? How are you?" She abandoned what she was doing and gave Ellie a big hug. "I'll put the kettle on. You get the biscuit tin out."

Ellie frowned. "I don't have time, sorry. There's a panic up in the office because the agency has let them down again over a replacement receptionist, and Angel has given me this *huge* list of things to do, and Zone One are coming in tomorrow, and—"

Sophie laughed, and held up her hands in protest. "So! A normal day in the Editorial Department then."

Ellie leaned against the table. "True. And," she said with a grin, "Zone One is the best boy band *ever*, and Al is my favourite. I can't *wait* to meet him! I have to keep telling myself not to think about it or I won't get anything done. But most of the jobs are away from the office, so no one will notice, will they, if I can't help thinking about him a *bit*?" She laughed. "Don't look at me like that. I'm not a *totally* lost cause. But yes, I ought to get on. Like I said, I don't have time to waste."

Sophie picked up the sack again and finished emptying it out onto the desk. "And I bet one of the jobs was to collect the post. If so, I'd better finish sorting it for you."

"So why aren't you delivering it like you

used to?" asked Ellie, looking around for the post trolley.

"Oh, it's just while I'm waiting for a new trolley," said Sophie. "Something to do with health and safety. I'm really missing my delivery round to all the offices. Instead I get a steady stream of people grumbling about having to come and collect their own post!"

"Well I won't grumble," said Ellie with a grin. "*And* I'll quickly help you finish sorting. I've got to take the post up before I can do anything else, so I might as well."

Together they soon had all the post sorted. There wasn't too much for *Heart's* editorial team for once.

"Are there any things on your list that I could help with?" said Sophie, as she slotted a last handful of letters into a box belonging to the marketing team for *Heart*'s big sister magazine, *Soul*, which was in the same building. "Sometimes I have a few quiet minutes, once all the post goes upstairs and before new letters and parcels start coming down for me to frank. It would be nice to get out for a breath of air."

Ellie paused. "Well there's Angel's dry-cleaning. It needs picking up from Shah's, just along the road. I don't have the ticket though. Maybe Piano's got it."

"Well if you can get me the ticket fairly soon, I could nip out and do that for you."

Ellie grinned. "Thanks so much. As a reward, do you want me to direct Zone One to the post room once they've been into the office tomorrow?"

Sophie laughed. "No thanks! You can keep them. They're not really my kind of thing. Besides, what would Flynn think?"

Ellie giggled. She knew very well that Sophie wasn't into boy bands. "Flynn would think you'd gone totally bonkers, wasting your time chatting to the members of Zone One."

"Exactly."

Ellie picked up the office post. "Thanks, Soph. See you later!"

Ellie hurried back to the office and handed Piano the post. "Do you have Angel's dry-cleaning ticket?"

Piano handed it to Ellie without a word, but as Ellie made her way towards Francesca with her post, Piano called her back. "By the way, as you're here, Angel said we could have proper coffee again. I hope you can remember our usual order?"

Ellie stared at her. It wasn't far to the coffee shop, where their usual order came from, but Angel and the others drank a *lot* of coffee – she'd be going backwards and forwards to the shop all day. It looked as if the list was going to grow even longer before she'd had a chance to tick any jobs off at all.

"Here!" added Piano. "You can take these to Francesca and Angel while you're around."

Ellie dropped the couple of letters Piano had

handed her onto Francesca's desk and took the rest through to Angel.

"Where's my coffee?" said Angel, without thanking Ellie for the post.

"I'm just going to get it," said Ellie with a sigh.

She dropped the dry-cleaning ticket off with Sophie and hurried out of the building. It seemed such a waste to send out for coffee when there was a perfectly good drinks vending machine in the office. But the staff all despised the machine, and only used it in a dire emergency. Ellie decided that while she was collecting coffee for them she might as well have one herself too. The coffee *was* very good, and she could drink it while she was finding out about collecting the shoes. She'd never been to a shoe designer's before. Would she get to meet the designer himself? What would he be like? And also, would she love his shoes?

3
Clothes and shoes

But there was a surprise waiting for Ellie back in the office. Francesca told her that she wouldn't be collecting the shoes today.

"Why not?" said Ellie, feeling rather bewildered. "Aren't they needed here for the shoot tomorrow?"

"Yes, they are," said Francesca. "But apparently Jacob Frou prefers not to let his shoes out of his sight overnight whenever possible. His assistant muttered something about insurance, but he does rather have a name for being a bit of an eccentric. It actually doesn't matter at all, but we must make sure you collect them in good time tomorrow."

"I doubt he'll let *you* collect them," said Piano balefully, looking down her nose at Ellie. "He'll think you're far too young and irresponsible."

"I *was* a bit worried about that," Francesca said calmly. "So I did tell him it would be you, Ellie. And actually he sounded charmed. So long as you take ID with you he said he'd be quite happy for you to accompany the shoes back to us in the morning." She frowned slightly as she looked at Ellie. "Do you know his shoes?"

Ellie shook her head. "I don't think so."

Piano rolled her eyes, but Francesca looked understanding. "This is his first collection for young people, so it's not surprising. I've always adored his previous styles." She sighed. "I'd love to catch a glimpse of his workshop and meet him. I expect you'll get to do both, Ellie, you lucky thing!"

* * *

For the rest of the day, Ellie worked really hard to get as many jobs done as possible. Between unpacking and hanging up some clothes for Angel to inspect, fetching coffee, and taking Ferdinand for two short walks – for which he was obviously very grateful – she spent ages typing up bits and pieces for the magazine. There was a backlog of readers' letters to type up, ready for the letters page, and there was going to be a feature on readers' pets, so Ellie had to extract and type up interesting snippets from *those* letters too.

It all took ages, especially as she had to scan in some of the pictures readers had sent to accompany the information. She felt very lucky to be allowed to choose the featured pets, although she knew that Piano or Francesca would cast an eye over the piece before it was passed for publication. Ellie didn't have to actually write anything – the page was going to be like a notice board, with photos pinned up alongside sticky notes with the comments on. Once she had done her bit, and her choices had been passed, the items would be sent to the Design Department. They would turn it all into one of *Heart*'s bright and interesting pages.

Just as she thought she'd finished, Piano threw a spanner in the works. "Don't forget to provide us with some extras, so when we reject some of your choices we've got others to look at."

"Okay. How many do you want?"

Piano tapped her crimson fingernail against her teeth, which set *Ellie's* teeth on edge. "About six ought to do it."

"Six! Francesca only wanted me to choose twelve altogether."

Piano stopped tapping her teeth and curled her lip. "Well then. Six will give us plenty of choice, won't it?"

As Piano sauntered back to her desk, Ellie glanced at her watch. She would have to hurry if she didn't want to work late, but she was determined not to leave finishing the job until tomorrow. She wanted to be seen as efficient and dedicated; and that meant staying until the job was done. And to be honest, it was no great hardship. It was fun sifting through and picking out all the most adorable cats and dogs – not forgetting the guinea pigs and hamsters. She'd even come across a picture of someone's stick insects. She hadn't been sure about including it, but at least it was unusual – and it was to hand, so now she most definitely would!

"Isn't it time you went home?" said Francesca at last.

Ellie uploaded the last picture and logged out of the system. "I'm just off," she said. "I've finished the pet thing, and done all the readers' letters too."

"Well done," said Francesca, looking pleased. "You've made a real difference today. I'm so glad you're back."

* * *

As soon as she got home, Ellie powered up her computer, and went online. Her friend Hannah was online too, so they had a good chat.

Zone One! You're going to actually meet them – you lucky thing!

Probably not for very long though, said Ellie. *We're sooo busy. But Francesca said she'll do her best to make sure we have a few minutes with them.*

We? said Hannah.

Apparently Piano loves them too, said Ellie.

Well don't let her ease you out, said Hannah. *You've got exactly the same right as her to drool over them.*

Ellie giggled. *I don't think Piano does drooling.*

I bet she will over Zone One! said Hannah.

Talking to Hannah made Ellie even more excited about meeting the boys. It was the chance of a lifetime to spend time with her fave band. None of her friends at school could boast of being so lucky. Ellie decided that she would ask the boys for their autographs. In fact... *Do you have their first CD?* she asked Hannah. *Or do you just have it as a download?*

Both! said Hannah. *I had to have the CD as well because of their picture on the front.*

Me too, said Ellie. *Well if you bring it round I'll take it to work with me in the morning and see if I can get them to sign it. I'm going to take mine. You'll have to promise to love me for ever though!*

*!!!****!!!* said Hannah. *Yes please!!! I'll be round in ten minutes!*

Okay, Ellie replied, but Hannah had already signed off.

In just a few minutes the doorbell rang, and Hannah was on the doorstep, clutching the CD. "You will be utterly, my very best friend for the rest of my life if you do this," she told Ellie.

"I'll do my best," laughed Ellie. "Now come in. You can help me decide what to wear."

In the morning, Ellie managed to catch an earlier bus, so she was at work in good time. Even so, both Francesca and Piano were ahead of her. Piano was wearing the highest heels Ellie had ever seen, and her hair had been put up, with wispy tendrils artfully arranged around her face. It looked as if she'd spent hours at the hairdresser's. As soon as she caught sight of Ellie, Piano rolled her eyes and pursed her heavily lipglossed mouth.

Ellie felt sure that Piano would never admit to having made a special effort to impress the Zone One band members, but it was obvious to Ellie that she had. Ellie longed to say something about the way they both looked. If Piano had been friendly they could have chatted about how much effort they'd both made to give a good impression, but she knew that Piano would never want to be any sort of friend to her. In spite of that, Ellie simply couldn't bring herself to say *nothing* about how exciting it was going to be meeting their favourite band. She pulled her CD out of her bag and waved it gaily at Piano.

"I'm all ready!" she said.

Piano rolled her eyes again. "You're not going to make a fool of yourself, are you?" she said. "You can't ask guests for autographs. Angel will be furious if you hassle them. The last thing they'll want is to be hounded by fans."

"Well you're a fan too!" snapped Ellie, feeling very cross. How dare Piano act so superior? Ellie marched to her desk and plonked herself down in her seat. But as she stuffed the CD back into her bag she began to wonder. Was it bad manners to ask people for their autographs? Would Angel be angry if she did? Didn't famous people expect it? She sighed. Trust Piano to make things complicated.

But she didn't have time to brood. Francesca, who was looking even more harassed than yesterday, was coming over.

"Don't get too settled," she said. "There'll be a cab coming for you soon. The main reception will ring up when it's here and Piano will give you a shout. All you have to do is go to Jacob Frou, collect the shoes and come back in the same cab. It's all arranged. Which is more than I can say for some things," she added under her breath.

"Will the cabbie have the address?" asked Ellie.

"Yes, of course. All you have to do is be in it, and look after the shoes on the way back. Now be ready. There's not much time." She hurried away, and Ellie closed her laptop, which she had just opened. It seemed weird to have to look after a load of shoes while they were in transit. What harm could they come to? The world of fashion and magazines could sometimes seem very different from real life, but that was what made it so exciting.

While she waited for the cab, Ellie checked the contents of her bag. Tissues, money, lipgloss, her CD and Hannah's, and her father's old notebook. The phone hadn't rung, so the cab couldn't be here yet. Maybe if she opened her laptop again and signed in that would make the cab arrive.

But the minutes ticked by, and still there was no sign of the cab. She watched as Joe Eagle, the photographer, turned up with his cameras. After a few minutes the Art Director came in too. She and Joe spoke for a few minutes and then they both went into Angel's office. Ellie felt awkward, as if it was her fault that the cab wasn't here. She was just about to go and ask Piano if it would be a good idea to phone the cab company again when Francesca came hurrying out of Angel's office with Joe and the Art Director in tow.

"Ellie! Why are you still here?"

Ellie stood up. "The cab hasn't come. I was just wondering if we ought to ring them again."

"Well of course we should! Piano should have done it before now. Piano!"

"What's the problem?" asked Joe.

Francesca explained while Piano rang the cab company. "They say they've been very busy but they should have one available in about twenty minutes," said Piano with one hand over the mouthpiece of the phone. "Inefficient lot!"

"Look, don't worry," said Joe sympathetically. "I can take Ellie over if you like. I know where Jacob Frou is – I did a job over there some time ago, and I've got to pick up a lens from the camera shop nearby."

Francesca looked relieved. "That's a brilliant offer, Joe," she said. Then she looked at Ellie. "Is that all right with you? You'll be quite safe with Joe. He'll look after you."

"That's fine," said Ellie. She liked Joe, and it would be much more fun chatting to someone she knew instead of spending the journey with no one except the cab driver to talk to.

In no time she was downstairs, and getting into a smart red sports car. She'd never been in a car with such low seats. It felt as if she was almost sitting on the road, separated from it only by the luxurious black leather upholstery. She felt very glamorous as they pulled out into the road, with the engine giving a throaty roar. Joe was a great driver, and Ellie settled back to enjoy having a ride in such a cool car.

"How do you fit your family in?" she asked, as the thought suddenly occurred to her.

Joe laughed. "Not in this car!" he said. "My wife has a people carrier that she drives during the week. At weekends, when I take over some of the ferrying around, we swap over. I couldn't get the kids' bikes in the back of this!"

Ellie looked behind her. There was just about space for his cameras, but not a lot more.

"So how are you enjoying learning about being a journalist at *Heart*?" said Joe, manoeuvring the car down a narrow alley.

"It's great being part of things," said Ellie enthusiastically. "I'm very lucky – especially today, with Zone One coming in!"

Joe laughed. "Famous people are always interesting to meet," he said. "And I've certainly met a few in my time – though I started off very much like you, running errands."

"Really?" said Ellie, wondering how long it took to get from office junior to being the owner of a smart car like Joe's.

"I can remember spending a couple of years in my first job lugging camera equipment around for my boss and hardly taking a photograph of my own. Still, it's all valuable experience."

"So who *have* you met?" asked Ellie.

For the next few minutes Joe told Ellie about all the celebrities he'd photographed. It seemed an impossibly glamorous life to Ellie, although it seemed it was just a job to Joe. Even so, it was one he obviously loved.

"Here we are," he said after a few more minutes, pulling out of the traffic towards the kerb. "Your destination, Ellie. Jacob Frou."

4

Monsieur Frou

In her haste, Ellie was already opening the door before Joe had quite stopped.

"Careful!" He braked hard, just before the door hit a lamp post.

"Sorry. Sorry!" Ellie was mortified.

Joe shook his head. "You're as bad as my kids. No patience. Never mind, no harm done. I'll just go and park the car, nip over to get my new lens, and meet you back here."

Ellie rang the bell by the door Joe had pointed out. There was very little to show that this was the premises of one of the most famous shoe designers in the world. The only hint was the modest *JF* in gold lettering on the door.

A voice crackled in her ear.

"Jacob Frou. Who is this, please?"

Ellie spoke into the entryphone. "I'm Ellie Ixos from *Heart* magazine. I've come to collect some shoes for a photo shoot this afternoon."

"Come on up."

The door buzzed and unlatched. Ellie pushed her way in and went up the steep stairs in front of her. At the top was another door. Ellie couldn't decide if she was supposed to knock or just go straight in. As no one answered her knock, she opened the door to find a large, light, airy room filled with an explosion of colours.

There were huge, bright sketches of shoes on the walls, a rainbow of coloured leathers stacked on racks, and boxes of all sorts of buttons, zips, beads and feathers on a large worktable in the middle of the room. Ellie longed to take a closer look at all the trimmings, but before she could move further into the room a young woman dressed in a beautiful green velvet coat appeared.

"Hi! I'm Bohemia. You've come from *Heart* for the young shoe collection?"

"Yes. I'm Ellie," said Ellie and she shook Bohemia's hand. "And yes, I have come for the shoes. They're going to be photographed this afternoon."

"They're almost ready," said Bohemia. "I've just been packing them up. We're very excited about this new collection. Monsieur Jacob has never designed for young people before."

"I'm sure they're lovely," said Ellie. "I can't wait to see them."

Just then the entryphone buzzed and Bohemia went to answer it. In a couple of minutes, Joe appeared at the top of the stairs.

"This is Joe, the person who is going to photograph your shoes," said Ellie.

"Oh yes, we've met," said Bohemia. "Hello, Joe. It's good you're here. Monsieur Jacob has been fretting about the shoot. Can you excuse me a moment? I'll go and fetch him." She disappeared into a back room. In a few moments she returned with an elderly man. He had a lot of pure white hair and was rather stooped. Ellie guessed at once that he must be Jacob Frou.

Jacob Frou and Joe shook hands. The designer obviously knew the photographer quite well. Immediately, Joe, Monsieur Frou and Bohemia got involved in a discussion about the shoot. The shoe designer had some very definite ideas about how his collection should be photographed, and Joe listened politely, although Monsieur Frou didn't seem to think that Joe was taking everything he said seriously enough. Ellie enjoyed looking round the studio while they talked, and just caught snippets of their conversation.

"No! No!" Jacob Frou sounded scandalized. "All my shoes must be worn! I don't want any photographed unworn. They need feet in them. And the right feet too!"

Joe tried to placate him. "But other designers—"

Jacob Frou drew himself up as straight as his bent back would allow him. "I am not other designers. If you cannot agree to make sure my shoes are worn for *all* the shots, I will not allow my shoes out of this workshop." He folded his arms and glared at Joe.

Joe glared back. "I'm just telling you how I've been briefed. I can make your shoes look beautiful, even when they *aren't* being worn by anybody."

Ellie shuffled *her* feet in an agony to be gone. Surely they hadn't come all this way to go back empty-handed? Whatever would Angel say if Monsieur Frou wouldn't let the shoes go and they couldn't have the shoot? He was appearing more and more agitated now, looking about him as if he'd lost something. At last his eyes fell upon Ellie, over by the trimmings. His face brightened.

"Take off your boots," ordered Monsieur Frou.

Ellie stared at him. "What? Me? Now?"

"Of course now," he replied testily. "How do I see them if not now? Do you want to be here all day?"

Ellie certainly didn't want that. "All right." She unzipped her boots and took them off.

"And the socks."

Under her boots she was wearing black socks, which matched her black leggings. Hastily she pulled them off and stood on the plain wooden floor in her bare feet.

"Hm." Monsieur Frou walked around Ellie as if she was a piece of furniture in a shop. "Give me," he said, holding out one hand to her. He obviously wanted Ellie to lift one of her feet up so he could see it more clearly. Ellie lifted her right foot up, and wobbled. Bohemia caught Ellie's arm and deftly drew a stool towards her so she could sit down. The designer took Ellie's foot in his warm, calloused hand and looked at it. "The Pirate. A five," he commanded, and Bohemia hurried away, to return a few seconds later with a pair of the most amazing shoes Ellie had seen in her entire life.

Bohemia kneeled on the floor and took Ellie's foot from Jacob Frou. Ellie almost felt as if they had forgotten that it belonged to her. Gently, reverently, as if the shoe was a priceless ornament, Bohemia slipped the right one onto Ellie's foot.

The soft leather of the shoe held Ellie's foot in a gentle caress. It looked a little like a pirate's swashbuckling boot, but instead of ending halfway up her calf, or at her knee, it hardly covered her ankle. It was decorated with braids and beads, and fastened with something that looked like an old and extremely valuable gold coin. Ellie couldn't imagine how the designer had done it, but he'd created the impression of a pirate's boot, while making it as light and delicate as a summer sandal. Ellie loved it. She wanted to demand the other shoe, so she could walk up and down in the pair. The shoe made her want to dance an elegant dance, though she had no idea how such a dance might go. The shoe made her feel a million dollars.

Jacob Frou looked at Joe. He pointed at Ellie's foot, fantastically enrobed in the Pirate, and then at the other, empty shoe in his hand. He was right. The shoe came alive when it was worn. Empty, it didn't have anything like the same impact.

"You see? My shoes must be always photographed on feet. I will come and speak to your Art Director, and if she will not agree there will be no shoot. Not one pair, not one shoe, away from a foot. You have models coming, yes? I know you do because we had their sizes emailed to us. So use them properly! No shots of girls holding shoes in their hands. I know what these Art Directors can be like."

He turned away from Ellie. Bohemia handed Ellie her socks with a friendly smile. "Lucky you! My feet are too big for these shoes, but I'd love to be able to wear them."

"Oh. Poor you," said Ellie with sympathy. Even though she was now pulling her boot back on, her foot could recall the gentle embrace of the wonderful shoe. Bohemia was right. She had been lucky. It had felt a great honour to model for its maker.

Joe came over to Ellie. "There's been a change of plan," he said. "Since Monsieur Frou has decided to come to the shoot, his shoes are going to travel with him and Bohemia in his car. There will be room for you if you want to go with them, or you can come back with me. It's up to you."

Ellie thought. It had been very kind of Joe to

bring her here, but her duty was to accompany the shoes. Even though she couldn't imagine that anything would go wrong if they were with their maker, she still felt uncomfortable at abandoning them. "I think," she said, "I ought to travel with the shoes…if you don't mind."

"Of course not," said Joe. "I had to come to pick up my lens anyway, and you're right to take your job seriously. Francesca should be proud of you. I'll see you later."

5
Short of time

Ellie looked at her watch. Time was ticking on. She knew that the boys from Zone One were expected at the office at midday, so that Angel could take them out for a quick lunch before the shoot. Bohemia was busy packing the Pirates back into their box. Ellie watched admiringly. She was sure she'd never manage to pack anything as neatly as Bohemia did those shoes. The designer's assistant used lots of colourful tissue, and was careful to make sure the entire surface of each shoe was well wrapped before it went into the box, which was lined with another vibrant layer of tissue. Once the shoes were in their box, tissue was folded over the top and the lid put on.

It seemed to Ellie that they must be ready to leave, but Monsieur Frou didn't seem in any hurry. He was sitting at his workbench, staring into space.

"What's he doing?" whispered Ellie, afraid of disturbing him. "He looks as if he's in a trance."

Bohemia smiled. "He is. Well, a sort of trance I suppose. He does this whenever he's thinking of a new shoe. If it goes well he'll begin sketching soon."

Ellie was appalled. She wanted to get back in plenty of time to meet Zone One before they went out to lunch with the Editor in Chief. What if she missed saying hello to Al? She wouldn't be able to bear it, and Piano would never stop gloating! "But we have to get back to the *Heart* office!" she said. "We don't have time for him to start new designs now."

Bohemia put her fingers to her lips. "There's

plenty of time before the shoot," she said quietly. "Don't fuss. Monsieur Jacob is an artist. When he's in the mood he has to work, and if he gets disturbed it takes longer. Come on. Let's go into the back room and leave him in peace."

Ellie followed Bohemia, feeling that she'd stumbled out of a dream into a nightmare. Didn't artists have any common sense? How could Jacob Frou even *think* of designing a new shoe now? But she knew that Bohemia was right. There was plenty of time...for them, but not for Ellie. Now that this had happened she wished she'd accepted Joe's offer to drive her to the office himself. She'd be almost back by now if she had. Instead, she was stuck here, waiting for Jacob Frou to finish designing. It was so unfair.

On the other hand, Ellie realized she could be wasting her father's advice to experience everything life has to offer. If she were

Francesca, she knew she'd be thrilled to be here while the master was at work. She *ought* to be thrilled, and at any other time she knew she would be, but at the moment all Ellie could think about was Al, and his floppy blond hair... and Piano, glorying in having the boys all to herself.

"Couldn't we take the shoes now, and leave Monsieur Frou to spend the rest of the day designing?" she said hopefully to Bohemia.

Bohemia looked scandalized. "I daren't do that," she said. "He's said he wants to be at the shoot, and to have a discussion with the Art Director. He'd get in a terrible temper if we left without him. Believe me, I know him better than anyone. We're best to sit it out here. I have some carrot juice if you'd like it, or a selection of herbal teas."

"No thanks," said Ellie, trying not to shudder. Carrot juice? Ugh! "It's very kind of you, but I just want to get those shoes back to the office."

"I understand," said Bohemia with sympathy in her voice. "But we really do have plenty of time. Monsieur Frou isn't going to let his shoes miss the shoot. He's far too sensible to do that."

Ellie watched as Bohemia calmly poured herself a glass of carrot juice and sipped it. Ellie looked at her watch again. Ten minutes had gone by. How long did it take to design a shoe?

After another fifteen minutes Ellie felt as if she was going to explode. She was very tempted to say that she was going to get a bus back, but Francesca had entrusted her with the job of bringing the shoes to the office. What if Monsieur Frou changed his mind about going to the shoot? What if he decided to work right through this morning, and on until teatime? What then? Would Bohemia be able to take the shoes, or would she have to stay with her employer? There was nothing for it. Ellie was trapped. She simply *had* to stay here. She had been sent to collect the shoes, and whatever happened, that was still her job.

Of course, if Ellie didn't get back until after midday, Zone One would already have arrived and gone out to lunch with Angel. There might possibly be a chance to meet them after the shoot, but equally there might not. Francesca had told her that the boys might need to rush off somewhere afterwards. Besides, they might well leave from the studio where the fashion shoots were done, without returning to the editorial office. Ellie started to chew her nails in agitation. She hadn't done that for ages, but she hadn't felt this stressed for ages either. How could she possibly bear to miss Al?

A few minutes later, the sound of classical music came from the workroom. Bohemia put down her half drunk glass of juice and got to her feet. "Good news. He's calm, and ready to move on. If it had gone badly he'd have put on some heavy metal." She poured a small glass of juice and gave it to Ellie. "There you are. Would you like to take it to him? When he sees you he'll remember straight away about the shoot."

Ellie took the glass, feeling hopeful.

Jacob Frou was still sitting at his workbench, but now he was hunched over, adding to some sketches on a large sheet of paper. Ellie drew close, and held out the glass of juice. For a few moments she thought he hadn't seen her, then he turned his head and looked up. "Aha! My young model. I think it is time we go to meet your Art Director, yes?"

Ellie smiled at him as she felt her spirits lift. Thank goodness! "Yes," she said gratefully. "It is!"

"You are anxious to go. So...Bohemia?"

"Here, Monsieur Jacob."

"Are all the shoes ready?"

"Yes."

"Then we will go. Hurry! I must make sure the shoot is done to *my* satisfaction as well as being right for the magazine." He picked up a silver-topped walking stick that was resting against his bench and tapped it authoritatively on the floor.

Bohemia grabbed a handful of large bags full of shoeboxes, and disappeared down the stairs. Ellie and Monsieur Frou followed her out onto the street. Bohemia hurried round the corner, but Monsieur Frou stayed where he was on the pavement.

"Shouldn't we follow?" said Ellie, thinking that he was dithering. She felt rather desperate at the prospect of having to shepherd the old man. But to her relief, Bohemia soon reappeared, behind the wheel of a huge, black limo. Ellie scrambled in and willed Monsieur Frou to hurry. It seemed to take him ages, but really it was only a few seconds before he was in, and Bohemia was closing the door.

The door closed with a satisfyingly expensive sounding clunk, and Ellie slid back in the soft leather seat. It was going to be all right. She would deliver the shoes as she had promised, Francesca would be pleased, she would get to meet Zone One, and say hello to Al. Hurray!

She breathed a sigh of relief, and looked out of the window. She'd never been in a limo before. It was a bit different from the bus, which was the way she usually travelled. It made her feel like royalty, or a mega-famous celebrity. She had to resist an impulse to wave at the passers-by. She fought down the laugh that was rising in her throat. Even if she *had* been a celebrity, waving would have been a waste of time because the windows were tinted so no one could see in! Instead she relaxed into the comfy seat and decided that this was one experience she could simply enjoy. Life could be tricky, and full of surprises, but here she was, bowling along in a huge limo, in the company of a designer whose shoes were going to feature in her favourite magazine. And she'd even tried one of his shoes on, especially for him. Honestly, all things considered, and with the excitement of meeting Al still to come, life couldn't get a lot better than this.

6
Shoes and Ferdinand

Ellie took the designer up to the *Heart* offices while Bohemia parked the car. As the old man gallantly held the door open for Ellie, Piano looked up and her eyebrows shot up to her hairline with surprise. "What have you done to Joe?" she asked.

Ellie almost burst out laughing, but managed to turn most of it into a cough. "This is Monsieur Jacob Frou," she told Piano with as much dignity as she could muster. "He has come to see the Art Director about the shoot. And Joe," she added, swallowing a giggle, "left on his own. I expect he's around somewhere. My job was to stay with the shoes."

"Well...fine," muttered Piano. She shot the designer a wide smile. "Welcome to *Heart* magazine," she said.

Jacob Frou hardly looked at Piano. Instead he spoke to Ellie. "You will make sure Bohemia is allowed up here?" he said. "Your security may not realize who she is."

"I'm sure Piano will ring down to tell the desk that we're expecting her," said Ellie. "And I can go down to bring her up." She looked enquiringly at Piano, who didn't exactly look thrilled at having to do anything that Ellie had the nerve to suggest, but then nodded her agreement and picked up the phone. Ellie couldn't help adding, "We left her parking the limo." She didn't feel the need to score points as a rule, but with Piano it was very difficult to resist.

Without waiting for a reaction from Piano, Ellie guided Jacob Frou to Angel's office.

At the door, Ellie knocked, and when Angel

answered she ushered Monsieur Frou in. "This is Monsieur Frou," she began, but Angel stopped her.

"I believe we have met," she said, getting up from her huge desk and advancing to shake the designer's hand. "Do take a seat. What a pleasure to have you here. Would you like a coffee?"

"Thank you, no," he said, perching on one of the powder blue chairs and leaning heavily on his stick. "I have come to see the Art Director about the shoot. My shoes must only be photographed on feet, not perched on shelves, or held. My shoes must be worn. This is essential, or the whole shoot is cancelled."

Ellie put the bags of shoes she was carrying down on the floor and left them to it. She knew that Piano wouldn't be able to leave the reception desk to fetch Bohemia, so she would have to go herself. But to her surprise, when she went back into the main office, Francesca was on reception, and there was no sign of Piano. As she made her way over to Francesca however, Piano appeared with Bohemia in tow. She handed Bohemia over to Ellie, and flounced back to the reception desk, grumbling under her breath.

When Ellie returned to the Editor's office with Bohemia, Angel seemed to be charming the old man very successfully. To Ellie's delight, she agreed straight away when he suggested that Ellie should help unpack a few of the boxes so that Angel could take a look.

In the past, Ellie had heard Piano being raged at by Angel for not being tidy in her office, and she didn't want to give the Editor an excuse to tell *her* off, so she folded the bags the boxes had been in very carefully, even though she knew that Angel probably wouldn't say anything while Jacob Frou and Bohemia were there.

Ellie lifted the lid off the first box. In a froth

of indigo tissue lay an explosion of light. Ellie lifted the shoe out in amazement. According to the label it was called the Dorothy. Putting on this shoe would be like plunging your foot into a basket of diamonds. Every centimetre was covered in crystals, including the small heel. There were two more boxes of shoes in the same style – Ellie loved the pair in sapphire blue. She could easily imagine going to a ball in shoes like those and wowing all her friends. When she unpacked the third shoe in the Dorothy style she could see why it had been so named. This one, in ruby red crystals, reminded her immediately of the red shoes in the film *The Wizard of Oz*. It looked entirely possible that they would be capable of granting any wish imaginable.

As she and Bohemia unpacked another box each, Ellie had to keep reminding herself to tidy as they went. It was tempting to let the packing tissue, in brilliant reds, greens, blues and yellows, billow around them as they worked. Such flamboyance suited the shoes. The collection was a wonderful celebration of excess. Ellie, sitting back on her heels and gazing at the delights on the floor was quite sure she would never be be able to explain to Hannah how wonderful it felt to be surrounded by such fabulous shoes.

Angel was cooing over them as they appeared out of the tissue, and the old man was calmly taking all the praise as his due.

"I think I ought to ask Francesca to take you and your wonderful shoes to the studio where the shoot will be," she said at last. "You will want to see it, I'm sure, and I expect Karen the Art Director is there now with Joe, so you can discuss the shoot before the models arrive. But could I keep a couple of these magnificent shoes with me for the moment? They are works of art, not simply footwear, and I'd love to have a few minutes to admire them fully."

Jacob Frou inclined his head in gracious agreement.

"Ellie, fetch Francesca for me, will you?" said Angel.

Ellie got to her feet and reluctantly left the sparkling collection. In the main office, Francesca was busy on her computer, but as soon as Ellie gave her the message she logged out.

"Are you all right?" asked Ellie, noticing her exhausted face.

Francesca gave Ellie a rueful smile. "I will be if we get to the end of the day with everything done properly," she said. She hurried towards Angel's office and Ellie watched her go.

"The band is going to be very late, so Angel can't take them out to lunch, one of the models is sick, and Francesca is probably going to be blamed for everything," said Piano helpfully.

"That's hardly fair," said Ellie. "It's not her fault." That would be just too cruel. After all,

Ellie knew that Francesca always had the best interests of the magazine at the front of her mind, whatever she was doing. In Ellie's opinion, blaming people, especially unjustly, wasn't the way to make people work harder or better.

"Angel doesn't worry about whose fault something is," said Piano. "She simply expects everything to be perfect, and if it isn't, people get told off. It would have been better if you hadn't brought the designer back with you. If he's here, it makes any problems more embarrassing for Angel, and that makes things worse for us."

"I didn't have a choice about that!" said Ellie. "I couldn't tell him not to come."

"No," said Piano, in an infuriatingly superior tone of voice. "I don't suppose *you* could."

Francesca was leading Jacob Frou and Bohemia out of the office. As soon as they'd gone, Angel called for Ellie.

"Tidy up, will you?" she said. "And when

you've done that, come back to fetch these. Someone can take them to the studio in a few minutes. I won't be long with them."

Ellie left Angel examining the shoes on the low table, gathered up the packaging and took it to the *Heart* lobby. She met Francesca there, on her way back from delivering Jacob Frou and Bohemia to the Art Director.

"All okay?" asked Francesca.

Ellie nodded. "Fine. Angel says she'll have finished with the shoes she's still got in a few minutes."

"Good," said Francesca. "I expect she just wanted to have a good look at the quality without the designer there." They had just reached the reception desk when they heard a loud scream coming from the direction of Angel's office. Ellie, Francesca and Piano exchanged bewildered glances.

"You were in there last," said Piano accusingly to Ellie.

"Let's go and see what's wrong," said Francesca in a resigned voice.

Ellie walked nervously with Francesca to Angel's door. She'd never heard the Editor in Chief scream before. But when they got to the open door, Ellie had to put her hand up to her mouth to stop herself laughing. Angel was chasing Ferdinand round her huge desk. The little dog was acting like a puppy, evading her every effort to catch him. Then Ellie saw what he was holding in his mouth and went white with shock. "He's got the Pirate!"

Something had got into Ferdinand. He was usually so docile, but the sight of all those shoes must have been too much of a temptation. He was galloping proudly around the desk with one of the Pirates held in his mouth, growling playfully as he went. Ellie, Francesca and Angel were all appalled.

"Catch him!" yelled Angel, sounding beside herself with fury. But her ire was aimed at Ellie.

"Whatever were you thinking, leaving them on that low table?" she demanded, as Francesca deftly cornered the dog and picked him up. She held him at arm's length away from her immaculate silk shirt and handed him to Angel. The shoe dangled from his teeth, but the fun had gone out of his game now he'd been caught. He let the shoe go without any prompting, and it fell to the floor before Ellie could catch it.

Quickly, she stooped to retrieve the shoe. To her great relief, apart from a small damp patch on the suede, and a couple of tiny tooth marks, it seemed pretty well undamaged. She put it on Angel's desk. Angel was standing behind her desk, clasping her dog and looking quite shaken, or maybe she was simply furious. It was difficult for Ellie to tell.

"You. Put his lead on and take him away. Don't come back until he's thoroughly exercised. If you neglect his well-being he's bound to become playful."

Ellie couldn't believe what she was hearing. How was it *her* fault that the poor dog was ignored? Angel professed to love Ferdinand so much, but really she treated the poor thing as an accessory. No wonder he felt like misbehaving occasionally.

Without a word, Ellie took Ferdinand's lead from the desk, and snapped it onto his diamanté collar. Angel put her dog down and glared at Ellie. "Off you go. And don't just drag him round the park. Give him some attention. And while you're out, take him to have his teeth cleaned. Tell Piano to ring the grooming parlour. They're sure to fit him in for me."

As Ellie left, with Ferdinand in tow, Angel was already completely calm. In her normal voice, she was talking to Francesca about a totally different subject. It was as if Ellie, and Ferdinand, had simply ceased to exist.

7

Time off

Ellie and Ferdinand made their way out after Piano had rung and found that the grooming parlour could indeed clean the dog's teeth. Before she let her go, Piano loaded Ellie up with several letters and a small parcel for Sophie to frank.

"Don't you run off now," Ellie warned the little dog as she dug around in the shoe cupboard for her trainers. But Ferdinand was quite content to wait now he was out of Angel's office. Ellie suspected that Angel would have a fit if she saw the trainers she wore while taking Ferdinand for a walk. No doubt Angel would insist on the highest heels for such a job. But Ellie didn't care.

She couldn't imagine that anyone would report back to Angel that they'd seen some sloppily shod girl exercising Ferdinand. After all, he wasn't exactly the most elegant of dogs. He was small, hairy, and his head was a bit too large for his body. If he'd been a Borzoi, or a Dalmation, Ellie might have felt the need to try to look as elegant as him, but Ferdinand, in spite of being owned by a cool magazine Editor in Chief, just wasn't in that league.

Down in the post room, Sophie patted him. "Not being used as a handbag today then, Ferdi?"

Ellie laughed. The first time she'd seen him she had mistaken him for a hairy handbag, as he'd been tucked under his mistress's arm. "No. We've escaped, haven't we? For a while at least."

"Have you met the famous boy band then?" asked Sophie, giving Ferdinand a broken bit of digestive.

"No." Ellie explained about her day so far, and the non-appearance of Zone One.

"So your Editor has abandoned the idea of going out to lunch with them then."

Ellie shrugged. "I should think so. But the photo shoot and interview are more important than lunch. I'm sure Angel can talk to them in her office if they're pushed for time." She laughed. "With luck she'll send me out to fetch sandwiches for them all. If so, I'll be able to say hello while I'm handing them out. Chicken tikka wrap anyone?" Then her face dropped. "As long as it doesn't all happen while I'm out with Ferdinand."

"I tell you what…"

Ellie looked at Sophie. "What?"

"I'll text you as soon as they arrive."

Ellie looked around the post room. "But how will you know, stuck down here? I don't mean to be rude, Sophie, but you're not exactly well placed to know what's going on."

"That's where you're wrong." Sophie smiled. "Steve in security will buzz me when they come if I ask him too. He's on duty today."

Ellie looked admiringly at Sophie. "I didn't know you were friendly with the security staff."

"I'm friendly with everyone," said Sophie primly. Then she grinned. "Steve and I got talking one day recently about what subjects his daughter is going to do at school. He's a big bloke, is Steve, and can look a bit intimidating in his uniform, but he's a lovely guy."

"Wow," said Ellie. "I always scuttle past feeling as if I must have done something wrong when he's around."

"Well now you know how nice he is you won't need to. He won't let us down. And there's no point in you rushing back. Take your time. I'm sure Ferdi deserves a break, even if you don't think *you* do."

"Well, okay," said Ellie.

"You won't be too far away to run here in time to see them, will you?"

"I suppose not." Ellie thought about it. "You're right. We're only going to the park – oh, and to get his teeth cleaned. I'll be able to get back in about five minutes if we sprint."

Sophie looked at the dog's short legs doubtfully. "*Can* Ferdinand sprint?"

Ellie laughed, and gave the dog a pat. "Well *I* can. I can always carry you if I have to, can't I, Ferdi? See you later, Sophie. And thanks!"

It might have been Ellie's ultimate ambition to work for a magazine like *Heart*, but after such a frantic morning it was also good to dawdle along the pavement, letting Ferdinand sniff every lamp post and litter bin that attracted his nose. She bought a banana at a stall, and ate it while walking, something else Angel would have hated.

In the park, Ellie strolled along with Ferdinand in tow, but once she was in the designated dog-walking area she could let him off the lead. While he sniffed around to his heart's content, and said hello to the other dogs, Ellie thought about the article she would like to write about meeting Jacob Frou. In spite of her panic about missing Zone One, the designer had made quite an impression on her. She could describe going up those narrow stairs, and arriving at his lovely, light workroom. And all those coloured leathers and trimmings had been fantastic. How she'd longed to dip her hands into the boxes of beads. She knew how expensive some of the trimmings were in her local bead shop, so could see that his workshop must have contained thousands of pounds' worth of materials. She'd noticed lots of foot shapes made out of wood as well. Maybe he used those to design on. She could imagine him cutting the leather, and stitching it, shaping it to fit. What an amazing skill he had – a bit like a sculptor.

Ellie sat on a bench while the dog snuffled around, and thought about being able to own a pair of Jacob Frou shoes, after the article she was thinking of writing was syndicated around the world and made her fortune. Of course there was the small matter of it not actually having been written yet, or asked for by *any* magazine, but it did no harm to hope, and to dream.

It was warm in the sun, and after Ferdinand had run about he was thirsty. So Ellie took him to the ice cream stand, where she knew a bowl of fresh water was always available for dogs. While he drank, she bought herself an ice cream. She was in such a good mood that she didn't even get annoyed when a little dripped onto her dress. She'd set out that morning so sure she'd meet Zone One. She'd taken her highest heels to wear in the office, and worn her coolest, retro minidress. She'd taken special care with her make-up and worn the most expensive perfume she owned. But after all that effort, here she was, mooching around in the park, with a scruffy little dog for company. She wondered if her dad had a phrase in his notebook for things not turning out as you expected. He probably did, she just hadn't found it yet.

Ellie finished her ice cream and called to Ferdinand. "Come on. We'd better go and get your teeth done."

In the dog grooming place, Pamper Your Pets, they were expecting Ferdinand.

"Your office rang up about it," the receptionist told the little dog, giving him a stroke. Then she looked at Ellie. "His usual pamperer is off today, but Sally knows just what to do. If you'd like to take a seat, I'll take him straight through...and while you're waiting, do help yourself to tea or coffee."

Ellie went through to the waiting area. Pamper Your Pets obviously believed that it was important for the owners to be well looked after, as well as the pets. The chairs were comfortable, there were china cups for the tea and coffee, and there was even a plate of yummy-looking Danish pastries under a glass dome.

There was also a collection of pink and black furry beds for waiting pets to sit on. There was no carpet, but Ellie supposed with a giggle that must be in case any of the pampered pets disgraced themselves. Washable floors were probably a must.

There was only one other person waiting – a man who was intently reading a dog magazine. After a few minutes, his dog, a large golden Labrador with an enthusiastic expression and wildly wagging tail, was brought to him.

It seemed to be taking rather a long time to clean Ferdi's teeth, so Ellie went back to the receptionist to ask if everything was all right. Angel would never forgive her if anything happened to her dog. The receptionist smiled at her reassuringly.

"Oh yes, everything's fine. He's such a good little dog. I think he's just gone in for his shampoo now."

"What?" Ellie stared at the receptionist, but before she could say anything else her phone bleeped. "Excuse me a minute." Ellie flipped open the phone and read the message.

Zone One just arrived. Be back soon! Soph xxx

Ellie's hand flew up to her mouth. She stuffed the phone back in her bag and looked at the receptionist again. "Shampoo? But I only brought him in for his teeth to be cleaned!"

The receptionist looked flustered. "Oh dear. I just assumed, when your office phoned, that Miss Makepiece wanted the usual for Ferdinand." She counted off the treatments on her fingers. "That's teeth, nails, shampoo, blow-dry and style."

"Well can you stop the shampoo?" said Ellie in a panic. "Maybe they haven't started yet."

The receptionist looked a bit put out. "Well I'll go and see if you like, but I'm sure he'll be—"

"Thank you," said Ellie, feeling like rushing behind the counter herself and grabbing the dog. Instead she had to wait, while the receptionist wandered into the back. She was gone for five long minutes, while Ellie paced up and down, trying not to bite her nails in her agitation. If they had already started bathing Ferdinand, how long would it take?

How long would the members of the band be in the office? Would Angel whisk them off for a late lunch after all, or would they still be there when she got back? Ellie was sure that once the band members went off to the studio for the photo shoot, although they would still be in the building, she would almost certainly have lost the chance to speak to them. And with a pang she remembered about her and Hannah's CDs. She'd so wanted to get them signed, in spite of what Piano had said.

The receptionist came back, looking sympathetic. "I'm sorry, but they've just put the first lot of shampoo on. We will waive the cost, of course, as you didn't actually ask for it to be done. But even if you don't want him blow-dried and styled it'll take a few minutes to rinse the shampoo off. It has to be done thoroughly, otherwise a dog's skin can become scurfy with the residue, and that can lead to irritation. I'm sure you wouldn't want to risk that."

"No!" said Ellie hurriedly. "Of course not."

"And then he'll need to be towel dried and brushed. Or we could do a combination of blowing and towel. He's got a thick undercoat, so it will take quite a while to get him completely dry. And then there's the brushing. You don't want him going home looking like a bottlebrush, do you?"

Ellie stifled a groan. The minutes were ticking by and she was stuck in Pamper Your Pets, while all the action was going on nearby. How could she bear it if she missed meeting her favourite band? Somehow, she had to get back to the office straight away!

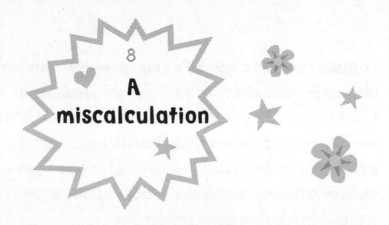

8
A miscalculation

The receptionist looked at Ellie sympathetically. She seemed to be weighing something up in her mind. "I suppose…"

"Yes?"

"Well, it's not a cold day."

Ellie willed her to go on.

"You could take him damp," said the receptionist.

Ellie's heart leaped. "Could I?"

The receptionist looked awkward. "Well, we wouldn't usually recommend it, but if you're in a hurry it's certainly possible: if we towel him a bit…to get the worst off."

Ellie seized the suggestion straight away.

"I expect by the time he's scampered back to the office he'll be dry as a bone," she said. "And I'll give him a brush later."

"Yes, you will need to brush him, and I expect his undercoat will still be...he won't get chilled, will he?" she asked, sounding as if she might be regretting her suggestion.

"No way!" said Ellie. "There's no need to worry about that. I'll keep him moving on the way back so he doesn't get cold, and once we're in the office, well..." She smiled at the receptionist. "He'll be in the lap of luxury. He's got a lovely basket with a good blanket in it, and our office is never chilly."

The receptionist smiled back, but still looked anxious. "Well, if you're sure he'll be warm enough. That's what I'd worry about. But I can see you want to get off. And after all, it was our mistake to shampoo him in the first place."

She disappeared again and Ellie could hear

her talking to someone in the back room. After a few minutes, she came back with Ferdinand on the lead. He didn't look *too* wet, and seemed very cheerful. It must be all right if they were okay about her taking him, and Ellie knew he'd be quite warm enough in the office. She just hoped Angel wouldn't notice he'd been shampooed when she hadn't asked for it. She would be bound to blame Ellie, although no way had it been her fault.

All of a sudden, Ferdinand shook himself, and to Ellie's horror drops of water sprinkled everything up to knee height and beyond. It seemed he was wetter than he looked. The receptionist raised her eyebrows, and then buried herself in her appointments book, as if she hadn't noticed. Ellie tightened her grip on the dog's lead, opened the door and hoped for the best.

It wasn't easy making Ferdinand walk on the lead. He kept wanting to stop and shake himself, and although Ellie supposed it was a good thing because it helped get him dry, it did slow them down an awful lot, and his behaviour also earned Ellie lots of resentful looks from dampened passers-by. One elderly lady even put her hand on Ellie's arm during one of the little dog's more vigorous shakes and remonstrated with her.

"*Must* you let your pet do that?" she asked.

"Sorry," muttered Ellie. "Come *on*," she urged Ferdinand. "You'll soon dry if you run."

They ran together, threading through the other pedestrians, and somehow managing not to get Ferdinand's lead tangled around anyone's legs. They ran until the office building came into sight, and then Ellie slowed to a trot. She didn't want to arrive too dishevelled, and Ferdinand was grateful to slow his pace, although he still seemed full of high spirits, wagging his tail enthusiastically whenever she spoke to him. He looked as if he'd enjoyed his time with her this afternoon, in spite of the unintentional bath.

As they went into the building, Ellie looked at him critically. He didn't actually look too wet now, although his coat was undeniably darker than usual, and he was becoming alarmingly more bottlebrush-like with every minute that went by. If she made him go to his basket straight away maybe Angel wouldn't notice. And with luck, the band members would still be there. Taking Ferdinand into Angel's office would be a perfect opportunity to meet them!

She told him to sit, and dropped his lead while she changed out of her trainers. Usually he was so good at waiting. Ellie had no idea what possessed him, but suddenly, Ferdinand took it into his head to run ahead of her into the office. Maybe it was an excess of enthusiasm after his afternoon out, or maybe he had missed his mistress. Whatever it was, it was a disaster. With one bare foot and wearing one trainer,

Ellie lunged desperately at Ferdinand's lead. "Come *here*, Ferdi!"

But it was no good. The lead slipped through her fingers, and Ellie was left sprawling on the floor. She got up in a panic and followed him. He was galloping through the office with evident enjoyment. Ellie clumped along behind him, hoping desperately that her trainer wasn't leaving dirty marks on the carpet, because Ferdinand's damp feet certainly were. She managed to kick off the trainer as she passed her desk. She scuffed it under her chair and hurried after Ferdinand in her socks. She was just in time to see him take a flying leap onto Angel's white silk lap, give his mistress a lick on her chin, turn round, jump off, roll energetically on the carpet with his legs in the air and a look of bliss on his face, and then hop into his basket with a very smug expression.

Into the ensuing silence came the big sigh of a little dog content with his lot, and the creak of his basket as he settled himself to sleep.

Ellie waited for the eruption that would be sure to follow from Angel, but it didn't come. And then she remembered Zone One. And indeed, there they were, all four of them – two on Angel's long, white sofa, and the others on the pale blue chairs – looking bemused...no, actually, she realized they were doing their best not to laugh. All at once she wanted to laugh too, but then she realized how she must look. In an office where only the highest heels and smartest clothes would do, she was in her socks, with an ice cream stain on her dress, and her hair a mess. No doubt her face was probably red too from chasing Ferdinand, and her make-up ruined. More than anything, Ellie wanted to look in a mirror, and tidy herself up a bit. But it was too late for that. One of the boys was speaking, and he was talking to her.

"Hi!"

It was Jay. He wasn't her absolutely favourite band member. Al, the one with gorgeous brown eyes and long, blond hair, was grinning at her from the white sofa, even better looking in the flesh than on TV. But she liked Jay too, especially the way he always seemed comfortable at taking the lead when they were interviewed. She liked that sort of confidence, but she felt totally lacking in it herself at the moment.

"Um...hi."

It was so unfair. She had been looking forward to meeting them all day. Now here they were, and she was a mess. "Excuse me. I must just..." Ellie beat a retreat. She retrieved her trainer from under her chair, horribly aware of Francesca watching, but saying nothing. Then she went past Piano, who was smirking, out into the lobby to finally put on her high heels. Before she went back into the office she went into the loo to inspect her face. To her surprise her make-up was fine, and her hair wasn't too bad, considering she had just been running. She scraped at the ice cream stain on her dress, but that was a lost cause. Luckily it didn't show too much. She sighed, and smoothed her dress over her hips. What on earth could she do to appease Angel? She couldn't think of a thing.

Ellie walked back into the office with as much dignity as she could muster. She made her way to her desk and sat down. She was sure Piano was laughing at her. Piano must have already had her few minutes' chat with the boys, lucky thing. She would have been on reception when they arrived, and Ellie could just imagine her chatting them up. But far worse than Piano's derision, and Angel's doubtless fury, was the knowledge that the members of Zone One, her favourite boy band in the whole world, were at this very moment in Angel's office and she had missed out on meeting them properly. There had been an opportunity for her to make a sophisticated entrance with Angel's dog, and hopefully get introduced, but she had made her entrance like a clown, thanks to Ferdinand's moment of madness. The grin on Al's face was frozen into her brain. Was it pity, embarrassment, or what? She didn't know – all she did know was that it certainly couldn't have been admiration.

And yet she couldn't really blame Ferdinand. *He* didn't know he was spoiling her entrance. As far as he was concerned he was just having fun. Perhaps he was just having a final blast, knowing that he would be expected to stay quietly in his basket for the remainder of the day.

Ellie opened her notebook, and her father's words leaped off the page at her. *Experience everything life has to offer.* Ellie wasn't finding that too helpful at the moment.

Francesca was very busy on the phone, and

didn't seem inclined to give her anything to do just now, so she tried to stop thinking about the band, and to start working on the article she hadn't been asked to write about visiting Jacob Frou. If she made a really good job of it, she could show Francesca and see if the Deputy Editor thought it was worth publishing. It would be wonderful if she said yes. Ellie was doing her best to look on the bright side, and be positive, but it wasn't easy, and she was very grateful to be left alone.

For a while she couldn't stop trying to listen to what was going on in Angel's office, but it was impossible to hear anything. She forced herself to concentrate on what she was doing, and after a while it became easier. There was a good article here, waiting to be written. She became so immersed, she actually missed Joe arriving, and was surprised when, a few minutes later, he emerged from Angel's office with the band members in tow. Piano was already preening herself, although Francesca carried on with what she was doing for a few more minutes. Ellie stayed where she was too, ducked her head, and watched the activity from under her fringe. The boys had gathered round the reception desk, and Piano was chatting energetically. At one point she glanced at Ellie and afterwards she and the boys all laughed together. Ellie was sure they must be laughing at her. She had never felt so miserable in her life.

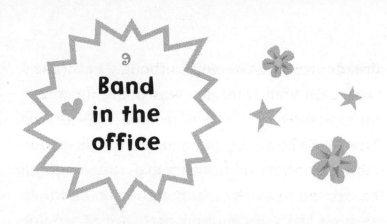

9
Band in the office

Ellie watched as Joe organized the boys around the reception desk, with Piano in their midst. It seemed they were going to take some casual shots of the boys in the office as well as the official shots of them in the studio with the models wearing Jacob Frou's shoes. Ellie had never seen Piano properly smiling before. In fact Ellie had wondered if she knew how. Piano could do a variety of smirks, and pitying glances, but a real, non-artificial sunshine smile was a novelty. It certainly looked as if she was having fun now, as Joe got her and the boys into position.

Ellie could remember seeing similar shots

of other stars in the *Heart* offices. She'd pored over them when they appeared in the magazine, often wishing she worked in such a glamorous place. And now here she was, with all the action taking place before her very eyes. She ought to be excited just to see it, but she couldn't help wishing she were more a part of it. Then Joe ambled over. "Come on," he said to Francesca and Ellie. "Aren't you going to join in?"

"You go," Francesca said encouragingly to Ellie. "Our readers will love seeing young Ellie in the pictures, won't they, Joe? They'll be so envious!"

Joe laughed. "I'm sure they will," he said. He looked at Ellie. "Come on then. The picture will look more balanced with two of you in it."

Ellie got to her feet, hardly able to believe what was happening. She was going to be photographed with the boys from Zone One! Then embarrassment made her hesitate. How could she bear it if they were still laughing at her? It would be mortifying. But Joe was in a hurry.

"Come on. The models for the shoes will be here in a few minutes, and I want to finish up here before they arrive."

Ellie followed him over to the reception desk. The boys were goofing around, asking Piano silly questions, and she was playing up to it big time. When she saw Ellie she sneered.

"Here's the dog walker wanting to get in on the act," she said. But if she'd expected the boys to follow her lead she was disappointed, and for once, Jay didn't speak first.

"Hi," said Al, ignoring Piano, and giving Ellie a warm smile. He offered his hand and she shook it, feeling instantly better. The other boys introduced themselves.

"I'm Jay," said Jay as if it was possible she might not recognize him. "And this is Matt and Ben."

Joe waved her into the group. "Stand

between Al and Ben, Ellie. Closer," he added. "I don't want to see space between you. That's better."

It felt very surreal, squashed between two such famous boys, especially Al. Never in a million years had Ellie ever dreamed she'd be this close to her idol, and he didn't disappoint. She could only see his profile, because he was looking at the camera, but it was totally gorgeous, even more fantastic than the many pictures she'd seen of him. She willed him not to look at her, so she could drink in his nearness without him seeing her stare, but Joe wanted them all to look at the camera, so she had to drag her eyes away. Piano was playing up to the other two, linking arms and smiling away for all she was worth. Ellie couldn't help a huge grin appearing on her face too. This was *sooo* cool.

Joe fired off a whole string of shots. "How about holding some of the CDs?" he suggested from behind his camera. Jay grabbed a couple from a heap on the desk and handed them to Ellie and Piano.

"And please look as if you love it," breathed Al into her ear.

"I *do* love your music," Ellie said indignantly, instantly forgetting to be shy.

"Really?" Al looked pleased, as Joe fired off a load more shots. "That's great!" His eyes met hers for an instant, and her heart felt as if it was quivering.

"Hey," said Ben into her other ear. "I loved your entrance earlier."

Ellie felt herself beginning to blush. The last thing she wanted was a picture of her in the magazine with a red face! She started to shrink away, but Al put his arm around her shoulders so she couldn't escape.

"How *did* you get the dog to do that?" he asked in an amused voice. "It was brilliant. Especially when he jumped into his basket at the end with such a satisfied look on his face."

"Your Editor's expression was pretty funny too," said Ben.

Before Ellie could think of how to respond, Joe interrupted them.

"Okay. Thanks, Ellie. Now let's do some shots with Piano chatting to Ben. You know the sort of thing – as if working here meant you got to chat to him every day!"

The group broke up, and Ellie's chance to speak to the boys was over. She was thrilled that she'd been included in a couple of shots, and she had managed to speak to Al after all, which was wonderful, but it was sad it had all happened so quickly. She hadn't had a chance to ask them anything, or reply to what Al had said to her. And none of them were giving her a second glance as she went back to her desk. Meeting them might have been a big thing for Ellie, but of course meeting Ellie hadn't registered at all for any of them.

Then Jacob Frou came back into the office with the Art Director, and made his way surprisingly quickly towards Ellie.

"That one!" he said, pointing his silver-topped stick at Ellie. "That's the one I want."

Meeting the band members had driven all thoughts of Jacob Frou out of Ellie's mind. She was surprised to see him, and couldn't imagine what he wanted. Then she remembered Ferdinand's antics with the Pirate. Had Monsieur Frou noticed the tiny marks, and come to remonstrate with her? But apparently not. After pointing his stick at her, Monsieur Frou made his way to Joe and tapped him on the shoulder, ignoring the fact that he was talking to Jay.

"I am a busy man, are you ready to photograph my shoes?"

Joe turned round and nodded at the old man. "I've just about finished here. Have the models arrived?"

Jacob Frou snorted in derision. "One has come, the other not." He lifted his stick again and pointed it in Ellie's direction. "Her feet, I like. So. Come." He beckoned Ellie impatiently. "Come!"

Ellie looked at Francesca, and Francesca shrugged. "Why not? I think you better had, as Monsieur Frou wants you. If it's okay with you, of course." Then she gave Ellie a little smile. "You've done well over the past couple of days, Ellie. And I'm sure it'll be fun. Go and have your feet photographed in Jacob Frou's shoes if that's what he wants." She lowered her voice, looking amused. "And you'll get to spend more time with your heroes too."

"Thanks, Francesca!" Ellie felt a million dollars. This was even better than riding in the limo! She grabbed her bag and followed Karen the Art Director, Joe, the members of Zone One, and Jacob Frou out of the office and towards the lifts. Piano had returned to the reception desk, with a face like thunder. She obviously wished she was going to be at the shoot too. If Piano had been a nicer person Ellie would have felt more sympathy, but as it was, she was a hard person to feel sorry for.

10
The sixth floor

Ellie followed the others, feeling a mixture of excitement and nervous anticipation. She had never before been up to where the studio photo shoots were done. The photographs of Ellie with Pop and Lolly Lowther had been taken in Angel's office. It would be really interesting to see where all the studio shots were done, but she was a bit nervous about what she might be asked to do. She'd never modelled before, not even when her school had had a fashion show a couple of years back, because she'd been in the wrong year group. All she wanted now was not to make a fool of herself in front of the boys again. Once had been quite enough.

However, Ellie had always been quite proud of her feet. They looked neat, and without burning, turned a delicate shade of brown in the summer. She had never thought they were exactly up to modelling standards, but Jacob Frou seemed to think they were, so she supposed they must be.

Then Ellie had a sudden thought. Would she be able to wash them first? She'd been running with Ferdinand while wearing her trainers. They were *bound* to need a wash. Then she told herself to relax. Surely someone would be in charge of such things. She might even get her toenails painted! And, whatever happened, it would be another new thing, in a day of extraordinary new experiences. She must enjoy it, and remember as much as she could so she could tell Hannah all about it.

The company that owned *Heart* magazine also owned a lot of other publications, and they were all housed in the same building. Ellie had been told that an area was available on the sixth floor for photography, but she hadn't known quite what the set-up was. As they emerged from the lift, she could tell that it was going to be impressive. A whole suite of rooms was in front of them. Karen led them past a small reception desk, and on into a long corridor. She paused, and waited for Ellie, who was at the back of the group, to catch her up.

"What's your name?" she asked.

"Ellie. Ellie Ixos."

"Right. Well, you go in there, and as soon as you're ready someone will bring you through." Without waiting for a reply, she led the rest of the group on along the thickly carpeted corridor.

Joe paused and gave her arm a pat. "You'll be fine, Ellie. They'll look after you in make-up and wardrobe. And I'm taking the pictures, so you don't need to worry about a thing. Just relax and enjoy it."

Ellie nodded, but as she wasn't absolutely sure what was going to happen she still didn't know if she ought to worry or not. She looked regretfully after Joe and the others disappearing down the corridor and then did as she had been asked, and went through the door that had been pointed out to her.

A cheerful-looking woman wearing a smart cotton tabard over her jeans gave her a welcoming smile. "*There* you are," she said. "Come on in and sit down. I'm Dawn." She drew Ellie towards a chair in front of a big mirror with lots of cosmetics arranged on a trolley nearby. "A ten, Sarah!" Dawn called towards an inner door. "Maybe an eight for the tops. Do you know your hat size?" she added, addressing Ellie. "It doesn't matter," she went on before Ellie could reply.

Ellie sat down politely, and turned to Dawn. "I thought they might just want to take pictures of my feet," she said awkwardly. "After all,

I'm not a proper model."

Dawn draped a bib around Ellie's shoulders and looked at a notepad on the shelf in front of the mirror. "Is your name Ellie?"

Ellie nodded. "Yes."

"That's fine then. Here for the shoot. Jacob Frou shoes."

Ellie nodded again.

Dawn smiled at Ellie. "So there you are. You might not be a proper model, but they've asked for you, and it's up to me to make you look like one. Don't worry!" she said when she saw Ellie's expression. "I didn't mean you were ugly, or anything like that! It's just that it's amazing how many little blemishes models have to cover up. What with that, and airbrushing the pictures afterwards, some photographs look nothing like real life. You're cool though. Hardly a blemish in sight! I'll have a look at your legs and feet once I've done your face."

Ellie gave herself over to Dawn's attention. She'd never had a makeover, or been to a spa, but imagined that it might be a little like this.

"Quite exciting, isn't it," said Dawn, "if you've never done this before?"

Ellie nodded, and Dawn put one hand on her head to steady her. She was already cleansing Ellie's face. "Do you like Zone One? I think they're fab."

"Me too," said Ellie. "I met them briefly downstairs."

"I can't wait to meet them," said Dawn with an excited grin. "I get to check their faces for shine. Lucky me! Now, what shall we do for you? I've got an excellent young range of cosmetics here," she told Ellie, "just right for your skin. Fresh summery colours, and no heavy foundation. You'll look just right for *Heart* magazine."

Once Ellie had relaxed, it was great fun having her make-up done. When Dawn had finished, she stood back and swivelled the chair, so Ellie could see her face in the mirror.

"Wow!" Ellie was thrilled. "My eyes look brilliant!"

Dawn had expertly blended several subtle colours to give Ellie's eyes fantastic depth. It almost looked as if she wasn't wearing make-up at all, but her eyes seemed larger, and the hazel colour of her pupils appeared to be much brighter. A spot that was appearing on Ellie's chin had been expertly disguised, and Dawn had put a summery, pink gloss on her lips.

Dawn looked pleased. "You can try doing your eyes this way at home, Ellie. Subtle blending is the trick to this look. And most people use far too much foundation. Choose the right tone, and then use the tiniest amount. Your skin ought to look as if it hasn't got anything on it at all. I can give you a little sample if you like. I'm always getting freebies from the cosmetic companies."

"Thanks!" said Ellie. "That would be great."

"Now," said Dawn, smiling at her again. "Hair next. We don't need to do a lot. It's in great condition. Just a bit of this so it doesn't get in a mess." She brushed through Ellie's long hair and sprayed it lightly. She looked critically at her and then nodded her satisfaction. "Perfect. Feet next. Can you take your shoes off for me, please?"

Ellie undid her shoes and took them off. Dawn was squeezing some cream onto her hands and soon she was rubbing it into Ellie's feet. Ellie did her best not to pull her feet away, but she did have terribly ticklish feet! While the scented cream soaked in, Dawn was choosing a nail colour for her. Soon Ellie had pinky red nails on her hands and toes, and Dawn was removing the bib.

"That's you then," she said. "Do you feel like a real model now?"

Ellie laughed. She certainly felt very

different with all the attention she'd had. "Perhaps I do," she said, admiring her pearly toenails. "Thanks so much. It's all brilliant."

"Glad you like it," said Dawn, sounding pleased. "Now, I really must go and get the shine off those boys' faces. You nip through to see Sarah and she'll fit you out with the clothes."

Ellie felt a million dollars as she went through into the next room. Today wasn't turning out anything like she had expected. She had thought it would be the best day of her life, but that had been when she had hoped to spend a few minutes meeting the band members if she was lucky. Now she was being turned into a temporary model for a shoot with them. How extraordinary was that? The last time she had appeared in the magazine, with Pop and Lolly, all her friends had been totally impressed, but this time, seeing her up close with boy band Zone One, they would go crazy!

Sarah, in the next room, presided over a couple of racks of clothes and a table full of accessories. She handed Ellie a pair of leggings not unlike Ellie's own and a stunning tunic top in a mixture of zingy colours. "Pop those on, would you? And then we'll get the shoes on."

It was lucky Ellie wasn't too shy, because there was no changing room. She supposed models got so used to constantly changing clothes for their work that they didn't think about it, but it did feel a bit odd. And Ellie's mum hadn't dressed her for years and years, but Sarah was twitching and tugging the leggings to get them how she wanted as soon as Ellie had them on, and she did the same with the tunic. For a few seconds Ellie felt annoyed. Then she told herself not to be so silly. Of course the clothes must be perfect, and it was nice that it wasn't her responsibility to make them that way!

Next, Sarah asked her to sit down. She took

hold of Ellie's heel and slid her foot into a wonderful pair of shoes that Ellie supposed might be called trainers, though the name by no means did them justice. The soft, green suede they were made of matched the green in the tunic, and when Ellie stood up, they were so comfortable she felt as if she was floating. Sarah adjusted the leggings at Ellie's ankles and then made her turn round.

"You'll do," she said briskly. "Through that door. Don't hang about after they've finished the shot. You've got three changes to get through this afternoon."

Ellie walked through the door Sarah had indicated and stepped from an ordinary, plain dressing room into a tropical paradise.

11

Photo shoot

The light was so strong, and the colours so bright, that for a few seconds Ellie simply had to stand still to get used to them. Of course the room wasn't really a tropical paradise. It was a photographic studio, but for a moment the illusion had been irresistible.

There was a bank of lights, shining as brightly as the sun, and there were silver umbrellas, bouncing all the light onto the set, where a girl and one of the members of Zone One were. There was a brilliant green, artificial palm tree on one side, and a couple of large beach balls on the other. The people seemed to be standing on a huge piece of bright white paper, which hung behind them like a backdrop, and continued on under their feet.

Then Ellie noticed Joe, busy with several cameras, and Monsieur Frou, who was sitting on a wooden chair out of shot, leaning, as ever, on his silver-topped stick. He looked keenly interested in the people, the set and the lighting, but most of all he was keeping an eye on his shoes. He noticed Ellie almost at once, and beckoned to her. She made her way over to him, making sure to remain behind the cameras and lighting.

"Let me look."

Ellie slowly turned round for him, so he could see the shoes on her feet from every angle. At last he nodded.

"Good." There was a pause. "Thank you for indulging an old man," he added. "Your feet in my shoes I like very much."

Ellie felt flattered but a little awkward. "Thank you," she said.

"You like the set?" he asked her. "They are going to make big feature out of my Pirate."

"It's amazing!" said Ellie. Then she hesitated. "But won't what I'm wearing look a bit odd with a desert island background?"

Jacob Frou laughed. "You see the white sheet they are standing on?"

"Yes."

"Watch, and you will see they change it to grey for your shot. Joe is taking close-ups, so you will not see the props in his pictures. They are for later."

Sure enough, as Ellie and Monsieur Frou watched, a couple of assistants changed the colour of the backdrop to a very urban grey.

The model was leaving, and the boys, who were all wearing crisp, neutral coloured shirts and pale trousers, were in a huddle, talking together and having sips of water out of bottles that had been standing ready for them on a nearby table. Joe attended to his cameras and then turned round and saw Ellie.

"Over here, Ellie. It's your turn."

Ellie went to join him, feeling suddenly rather shy, but Joe didn't give her a chance to worry about that.

"Okay. Now, I want you to sit on the floor there, and one of you – Jay? – to sit nearby, at an angle to Ellie. That's it. A bit further away. Right." He went back behind his camera and looked through the viewfinder. "Okay. Now, Ellie, put one of your feet on Jay's shoulder and Jay, hold her other foot in your hands. Put your hands behind you on the floor, Ellie. Otherwise you'll fall over!"

Ellie couldn't help giggling, but Joe liked that. "Brilliant! That's going to be a good, fun shot. Now try having one foot on the floor and the other in Jay's hands. Great! Jay look at Ellie."

Jay looked at Ellie and made a face. Ellie

burst out laughing. She simply couldn't help it, and when Joe asked her to look at the camera, she did so with such a happy, carefree expression Joe was very pleased indeed.

"We'll make a model out of you yet," he told her as they paused between shots.

"But I'm going to be a journalist," she told him.

"Ah! But there's nothing like experiencing different things to give you ideas for articles," he told her.

"That's true," she agreed.

Then Ellie had to get changed for the next pair of shoes. This time she was with the young model, who was very professional indeed. She helped Ellie a lot with the shots. They were photographed on a green background with arms linked, as if they were going for a walk in the sunshine. The model, whose name was Milli, could put on any expression asked for, and still look totally genuine. She also worked very quickly, without needing lots of instructions, which Joe obviously appreciated.

Then, while they went to get changed for the Dorothy, Joe took some studio shots of the band. Al looked even more gorgeous under the bright lights than he had in the office, and Ellie realized that they'd all had their hair styled, as well as Dawn having taken the shine off their faces. She wished she could watch them having their pictures taken, but she and Milli were stuck in the back, changing into short, silky dresses – red for Milli and blue for Ellie. While Sarah was fussing over them, Ellie asked Milli how old she was.

"Fourteen," said Milli with a grin.

Ellie was very impressed. Milli was the same age as her, and yet already had a glamorous career!

"How do you fit in schoolwork?" she asked. "Do you even *go* to school?"

"Yes," said Milli. "I go to one here in London.

I get time off for my job, but I have to study hard to keep up with the rest of the class. I wouldn't want to give up school even if I could though," she went on as Sarah fastened the buckles on her red Dorothy shoes. "I want to go on to university, so there's no way I'm going to neglect my lessons."

Now, Ellie was even *more* impressed, but Milli seemed to think that Ellie had her life pretty well sorted too. "I should think it's *sooo* hard to get onto a magazine like *Heart*," she told Ellie. "You must be seriously good."

But there was no more time to talk. They had to get back out onto the set, where the boys were waiting. They'd changed out of their neutral shirts into silky ones in colours that were pale echoes of Milli and Ellie's vibrant dresses and shoes. Jay and Ben were in red, while, to Ellie's great delight, Al and Matt were in blue. This time, Joe wanted them to pretend they were going to a party, with the four boys accompanying them. "Oh my!" said Milli with a giggle. "Won't all the readers envy *us*!"

The white backdrop behind them made them stand out brilliantly, and their Jacob Frou shoes positively *sparkled* under the lights. Ellie tried not to look at the blinding spotlights in case her eyes started to water. She didn't want to spoil her fantastic eye make-up.

"Okay, boys. You have one girl between two. No fighting now!" Joe had the knack of saying just the right thing to get the mood perfect. The boys immediately began pretending to argue, and Joe banged off lots of shots while the girls laughed at their antics. Then Matt took Ellie's hand, as if to lead her off to the dance floor. But Ellie was wishing Al had got there first. She glanced back at Al and he looked straight into her eyes. Ellie just melted and at that instant Joe snapped off another shot. Ellie hardly noticed. The silky feel of the wonderful dress she was wearing, the amazing shoes sparkling on her feet, and Al from Zone One gazing into her eyes had distracted her. She was sure she was falling in love!

The last shots were to be of the Pirate. Ellie and Milli were put into strappy, striped tops, with Milli in cut-offs and Ellie in a short, swinging skirt. At the last moment, Sarah popped a wide pirate hat onto Ellie's head. Ellie had never liked wearing hats, and there was no time to look into a mirror to see what she looked like, so she simply hoped for the best.

The cameras had been pulled back, and the white paper rolled away, revealing a sandy yellow background. There was a messy pile of piratical props to play around with. Ellie was feeling a bit shy of Al now, since meeting his eyes in the last shot, but he picked up a toy telescope, pointed it at her and said, "I see no hardships!" That made her laugh, and her tension dissolved.

An assistant wheeled in a large box, painted

to look like a pirate's treasure chest. Spilling out of it amongst a froth of tissue were almost all the Jacob Frou shoes. Amongst them Ellie could see the three different colours of the Dorothy, the green shoes she'd modelled earlier, and several others. *But Monsieur Frou didn't want his shoes photographed unless they were on feet!* Ellie looked anxiously over to where Jacob Frou was sitting, but he seemed perfectly happy. Could it be that the Art Director had been able to change his mind about that? Certainly the shoes were fantastic masquerading as treasure. The boys looked pretty good too. Jay was sporting an eyepatch, and Al was wearing a pair of huge, turned-down boots and, like the other three, a stripy T-shirt.

For one of the shots, Joe got Matt to pick one of the sparkly shoes out of the box and for Milli to pretend to try and snatch it from him. Ellie looked over towards Monsieur Frou again, but he was watching with a pleased expression on his face. Obviously he *had* changed his mind, thank goodness. Karen and Joe must have persuaded him that they knew what they were doing. And the Pirates, which he had so objected to being seen unworn, were on Ellie's and Milli's feet, not in the treasure chest, which was maybe what had swung it for Monsieur Frou.

All too soon the shoot was over. Joe professed himself happy with the shots he'd taken, the lights were switched off, and Ellie and Milli went back to change out of the borrowed clothes. While they were getting changed they promised to find each other on Facebook very soon. Milli's mum arrived to take her home and Sarah was clearing away the clothes. Bohemia was there too, packing all the shoes back into their boxes.

"Dawn had to go, Ellie," said Sarah. "Did you want to take your make-up off? She left some things out for you if you did."

"No, it's all right," said Ellie. "The look she's given me is so fab I can't bear to take it off. I'm going to keep it on until my mum and my best friend have seen it."

Sarah laughed. "Well she's certainly done you proud," she said. "Did you have fun, Ellie, being a model for a couple of hours?"

"Yes!" said Ellie. "It was fantastic. I'm not sure I'd want to do it all the time though." She looked apologetically at Milli. "It's a great job, but just not for me."

Milli grinned.

"Meeting the boys from Zone One was pretty cool, don't you think?" said Ellie.

"Yes!" said Milli. "I had no idea that was going to happen. They were really nice, weren't they? Oh, my friends at school are going to be so envious!"

"Mine too," said Ellie.

Milli gave Ellie a quick hug and then she was gone.

Everything was being shut up in the photography suite. Dawn had left out a couple of samples of foundation in a sweet little bag, with a note for Ellie. *Enjoy!* it said. Ellie happily picked up the bag after peeping inside. There had been so much excitement today and she had a goodie bag to take home too. It felt like the most wonderful sort of party, even though she supposed it had been work really, of a kind. Except...now the excitement was over, she was conscious of a rather big hole where her stomach used to be. Then she remembered: she had managed to eat a banana and an ice cream, but she could hardly call that lunch! She really ought to go out and get herself a sandwich, otherwise she'd never survive for the rest of the day. Ellie headed for the lift and was soon being taken back down to the third floor.

She imagined how sober it would seem in the office after all the bright lights and chatter in the studio. Modelling seemed to be a bit like acting. In front of the camera, Milli appeared very slick and professional, bringing any expression asked of her to her face immediately, and holding any pose required with apparent ease. In the changing room though, she was just like any other normal fourteen year old, swooning over Zone One. And what about Zone One? Were they just normal boys really, apart from being so famous, of course? Ellie wanted to know what it was really like being famous. Was it possible to keep old friends from beforehand, or did it all get too celebrity-minded and complicated? She had heard famous people described as down-to-earth and grounded, but was that really possible when you had countless people telling you how wonderful you were?

The lift stopped and the doors opened. To her surprise, Ellie was greeted with a hubbub that she certainly hadn't expected. There was no sign of Karen or Joe, but the members of Zone One were there, all chatting to Piano, and Jacob Frou was making his way towards the door, with Bohemia carrying a load of bags in his wake. It seemed the day wasn't quite over yet.

Monsieur Frou smiled at Ellie. Then he frowned, and looked back at Bohemia. "The box."

Bohemia looked puzzled for a moment, and then her expression cleared. "Of course." She put her load of bags down and disappeared back into Angel's office. In a moment she returned, carrying yet another of the shoeboxes, which she gave to Monsieur Frou. He opened it and rummaged about amongst the tissue for a few moments, looking at what lay inside. Then he grunted, and replaced the lid.

"For you," he said to Ellie, and to her astonishment, thrust the box into her arms. "You didn't complain. You did a good job.

Thank you." He looked at her feet, encased in her office shoes and grunted again. "Look after your feet," he told her. "They are the only ones you've got. Come on, Bohemia. We must go."

"I will," said Ellie as he began to move off. "And..." She raised the box in her hands. "Thank you!"

Bohemia gave her a grin as she passed. "Enjoy them!" she said.

Once the old man and Bohemia had gone, the boys crowded round Ellie. "What's he given you?" said Jay.

"Open it!" said Ben.

Piano was pretending not to care what might be in the box. "It's probably a bottle of foot balm," she said dismissively.

Ellie put the box on a corner of the reception desk. Holding her breath, she took off the lid. Inside was a profusion of dark blue tissue. She could see a glint of gold underneath. She felt her heart race.

"Go on," said Al at her shoulder, quietly urging her. "Take them out."

With her heart in her mouth, Ellie parted the tissue and looked in. She gasped. Suddenly, it was like all her Christmasses and birthdays rolled into one. There, nestling amongst the navy blue tissue, was what she had hoped for more than anything: a pair of the Pirate!

For a moment Ellie thought she might cry. They were such a *wonderful* gift. She lifted one out and gazed at it. These shoes would be a fantastic reminder of an extraordinary day. Hadn't Monsieur Frou himself chosen the Pirate especially for her feet back when he'd first met her in his workshop? He'd known what suited her best. Ellie couldn't imagine that many people had shoes personally selected for them by the designer. She would treasure them for ever.

Piano had glanced at the shoes, sniffed, and was now bending to pick up her bag before leaving, but Francesca had a smile on her tired face. "Am I right in thinking this is your first bit of designer wear?" she asked.

Ellie nodded.

"Well," said Francesca, "while working at this magazine, I'm sure there'll be more to come. But there's nothing like your first piece, and those shoes are exquisite. Don't be afraid to wear them though. You wear them and enjoy them. That's what they're made for. Well done, Ellie."

12
A meal out

"Put your new shoes on," said Al in her ear.

But before Ellie could take them out of the box, Francesca was speaking to her. "Angel wants to see you in her office," she said. "You can try your shoes on later."

Casting Al a regretful look, Ellie went to see Angel. She was sitting behind her desk. "I think you wanted to see me."

Ellie's mind went blank. "Sorry?"

Angel tightened her lips. "That is an appropriate thing to say. The correct answer is yes."

For another moment Ellie had no idea what Angel was on about...then it hit her. She glanced at Ferdinand, lying innocently in his basket, with his coat looking more than usually fluffed up, and back to Angel, who had changed her clothes since Ellie had last seen her.

She felt a blush working its way up her neck, over her face and into her hairline. "Oh yes. I am sorry about that, Angel. I didn't ask for Ferdinand to be washed though. They did it without telling me..."

Angel wasn't interested in listening to excuses. "When I ask you to do a job, I expect that job to be done."

"Yes, Angel."

"And when the unexpected happens I expect you to use your common sense to work out how to get round it. I don't expect you to come rampaging in here with a wet dog."

"No, Angel."

"And if you think I don't realize that you rushed back here solely to see those four boys –" she paused and fixed Ellie with a steely gaze – "you're not as intelligent as I thought you were."

Ellie bit her lip. "No, Angel."

Angel Makepeace pushed a rectangular piece of plastic towards Ellie. "While you are working for *Heart*, the magazine is the most important thing. Which is why, instead of sending you home, I want an article out of you."

Ellie nodded eagerly. "Of course, Angel. Anything."

"An account of your day with the band. Emailed to me without fail by tomorrow afternoon. And give this to Francesca. Don't let me down, will you?"

Ellie picked up the credit card Angel had passed her and held it tightly. "No, Angel, I won't let you down. I promise."

"All right then. Just don't ever *ever* bring my dog back into my office in that state again. In future, I don't care how long it takes you, but he must be clean, and completely dry."

"Yes, Angel. I promise."

It seemed the Editor in Chief had no more to say, so after waiting a couple more seconds, Ellie retreated. She closed the door quietly behind her and took a deep breath. Thank goodness no one had been around to witness *that*. So much had happened today that she'd forgotten all about Ferdinand's unwanted shampoo. Well, at least Angel hadn't said that she didn't want Ellie to show her face in the office again. And she was quite within her rights to be angry. Ellie took the credit card to Francesca, feeling as if, on balance, she'd had a very lucky escape.

"Thank you," said Francesca, tucking the card into her bag. "Now hurry up if you want to wear your new shoes. The car's waiting."

"Sorry?"

"You want to come and eat with us, don't you?" said Francesca. "Everyone else is starving.

And it'll be good for your article, having a meal with Zone One."

Ellie was a total mixture of emotions. So Francesca knew about the article Angel wanted her to write, and probably about the telling-off she'd just received too...that was embarrassing. But she was getting to go out for a *meal* with Al and the others...that was beyond amazing!

"Well go on," said Francesca, with a slight smile. "Get those shoes on."

"Yes!" said Ben, wandering over to them. "Wear them out to eat with us. They look so great."

"So are you joining us then?" said Al as Ellie scrambled to put on her Pirates.

Piano rolled her eyes. "She's just a child," she told the boys. "She's too young. She'd need to ask her mummy."

Al looked a bit annoyed. "But not childish," he replied mildly.

Piano didn't look at all pleased at that. She looked even less impressed when Francesca stood up for Ellie too.

"Ellie is staff," she told Piano mildly. "Of course she's coming. Phone your mum if you want to," she added to Ellie. "But you shouldn't be late home."

If anything could have spoiled Ellie's mood it might have been the realization that Piano was going to be joining them. But nothing could alter Ellie's feeling that the day had gone from good, to great, to fantastic! Going for a meal with Al and his fellow band members was a dream come true for Ellie Ixos!

Piano was still looking grumpy as they went down in the lift and piled into a large people carrier with blacked-out windows, but she didn't seem to mind being squashed next to Matt too much. It only took a few minutes for the car to reach the restaurant, and when it did, Ellie had a sudden panic about money. Surely the food would cost a fortune! Did she have enough cash on her to eat *anything*? But Francesca soon put her at her ease.

"The meal is on the magazine," she told Ellie quietly. "That's why I've got the company credit card. You can choose what you like."

It was far too early for dinner, and *very* late for lunch, but the restaurant had been warned, and were ready for them. Ellie found herself sitting between Al and Jay at the table, which meant she was in seventh heaven. She didn't forget about the article Angel wanted though, and tried to think of good questions to ask them.

"Do you often get to eat out like this?" she asked Al.

"Not often at the moment," he said. "We've been in the studio a lot recently, finishing the album. We usually get food sent in while we're there. And then we're going on tour soon, so that'll mostly be hotel food in our rooms,

I expect. This is cool. It's great having a meal without people coming up and asking us for our autographs all the time."

"Oh."

Ellie remembered about the CDs she had in her bag and wondered what to do. She'd promised Hannah, but now she knew that Al at least would rather not sign autographs. She wished she'd proffered the CD earlier, before she'd known the truth. But then he might have been annoyed. Sometimes life could be very tricky. Maybe he wouldn't mind after the meal, just before they parted...if she didn't actually badger him. She'd have to see. But it seemed he'd noticed her fallen face.

"Don't get me wrong," he said. "We *love* signing for people usually. It's just nice not to occasionally."

"That's a relief," said Ellie. "I've got a couple of your CDs in my bag, but I didn't want to ask if it was going to annoy you."

Al leaned in and whispered in Ellie's ear. "I'd sign for you *any* time," he whispered.

Ellie felt as if she was melting all over again and she found herself giggling to cover her feelings.

"What are you laughing at?" asked Al, laughing too.

"Nothing," said Ellie, trying to stop. "I'm just enjoying myself."

"You're as bad as my sister," said Matt, who was sitting opposite her. "She's always giggling. If I'm not careful I start giggling too. Then neither of us can stop."

One glance at the expression on Piano's face made Ellie want to giggle even more. Piano looked furious when Matt spoke to Ellie. She seemed to have decided that Matt was her favourite, which meant that Ellie shouldn't speak to him, but no way was her expression going to put Ellie off. Besides, she had her article to think about. She couldn't stop talking to any of the boys just to please Piano.

"I thought you didn't eat meat," said Ellie, overhearing that Al and Matt were going to order steak.

"You've been reading up about us," said Al with a grin.

"You can't believe everything you read," said Matt. "We did try being vegetarian for a while, but we like meat too much."

Ellie laughed.

"We're always being asked stuff," Al explained. "And we can't always remember what we've said. I expect you change your mind about things from time to time."

"That's true," said Ellie, feeling in her bag for her phone. She'd just decided that she ought to text Hannah about what she was doing. It would be fun to put the text in the article, as well as Hannah's response to it. While she was about it she thought she'd send the same text to her mum to let her know what she was up too. Al looked a bit concerned when she opened her phone.

"You're not going to tell your mates where you are, I hope, because if you do that and they pass it on we'll end up with loads of people arriving to gawp at us."

"No way!" said Ellie. "No. I was just letting my friend Hannah and Mum know what I was doing." She explained about the article she had to write. "I thought it would be fun to get a real response from Hannah," she explained, "rather than make one up. You can see the text if you like."

Al peered over her shoulder and read the message aloud. "*Having a meal with* Heart *staff and Zone One! Tell you all about it later.* That's okay," he said. "Sorry to be so paranoid, only it's fun not having any fans around for a change."

Except me and Piano, thought Ellie as she sent the text. In no time an answer came back.

You lucky thing!!!! Give Jay a snog from me.

Don't forget to get the CDs signed. I am soooooooooo jealous.

"Let's have a look," said Al.

"It's embarrassing!" said Ellie, trying to close the phone, but Al was too quick for her.

"Ha! So Jay is her favourite is he? Shall we get him to send her a kiss on your phone?"

Ellie laughed. "Go on then, if you like. She'll be totally overcome."

"Do you get free picture texts on this phone?" asked Al.

"I've got quite a few left," said Ellie. "Why?"

"We can take a pic of Jay blowing her a kiss, and send that to her as well as a text," said Al with a grin.

"Oh wow!" said Ellie. "That will make her entire life!"

It only took a few seconds to take a picture of Jay. Ellie sent the picture and text with a giggle. "I can't imagine what she'll say in reply," she said.

In a couple of minutes Hannah's response was clear.

!!!!!!!!!@@@%%%$$$***xxxxxxxxxxxxxxx xxxx

Jay pretended to be worried. "Does that mean she's annoyed?" he said.

Ellie couldn't stop laughing. "I think it means she's my friend for life," she said.

When a reply came from Ellie's mum it was much more sedate.

Good for you! Have fun, and behave yourself. See you later, Mum xx

Ellie smiled and put her phone away.

The waiter who took their order didn't show any signs of recognizing the band members, but while they were waiting for their food, Ellie noticed a couple of customers staring at them. She glanced at the boys, but they didn't seem to have noticed. When the food arrived however, it was brought by a waitress, who spent ages fiddling around with their plates, drinks and cutlery. Ellie was sure that the waitress must know who the boys were. She looked as if she badly wanted to say so, but managed to restrain herself. Ellie felt full of sympathy. She was sure that if *she* was a waitress and had to serve someone famous she'd find it *impossible* not to say hello.

Eventually, the waitress didn't have an excuse to hang around any longer, and was forced to leave them to eat while she served other tables.

"What do you do when people stare at you?" Ellie asked Al.

"Ignore them until they come over and say hello," he said, helping himself to more vegetables.

"Does it get annoying?"

Matt took a long swig of his drink and set it back down, steadfastly keeping his gaze away from the other customers, and joined in the conversation.

154

"It's funny," he said. "When we first became famous we thought it was great. All that attention! People want to give you things, they tell you how brilliant you are, all that stuff. But you soon get tired of it. We're very grateful that we're so popular, but you lose something by being famous. Simple things like this –" he gestured at his meal – "can become difficult."

"But you can't beat eating out for a change," said Ben. "Even if there is a risk of being mobbed before the end of the meal."

"Damn!" said Al. "There are a couple of people at the table by the window busy texting. They *might* not be texting about us, but they keep looking over. I reckon they've clocked us. And if those texts *are* about us we might be getting some company pretty soon."

Piano let out a squeak of alarm, stabbed a piece of celery onto her fork and put it into her mouth. Ellie swallowed, and took another bite of her chicken.

"It'll be fine," said Jay soothingly. "This restaurant is very good about keeping people at bay on their premises."

Ellie was sure Al must be right. The people at the table in the window probably were texting their friends about the band. She could imagine how quickly the news might spread, and felt a bit anxious. Then she felt Al's hand on her arm.

"Don't look so worried," he said. "It's no problem. You've got nothing to be concerned about and, just think, if by any chance there are fans waiting outside by the time we go, it'll be great for your article. You'll get to find out first-hand what it's like to be famous!"

"That's true," said Ellie, hoping that there *would* be some fans. It would be fantastic to be able to write about that!

Just then, a gaggle of young people burst in through the door of the restaurant, laughing, and looking hyped-up and excited. They stared openly at Jay and the rest of the band, while the band studiously pretended not to have seen them. The six young people were soon approached by a couple of waiters and the manager who, with very little fuss, guided them back outside.

Al grinned at Ellie. "See what I mean?"

Ellie did see. The restaurant seemed well able to deal with anyone who was inclined to be a nuisance. She relaxed. She had to admit to herself that the whole thing was rather exciting. She knew of course that it wasn't *her* that people were interested in seeing, but to be a little part of such attention...well, it was *fun*!

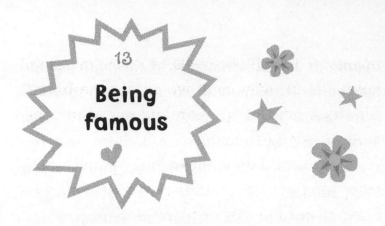

13

Being famous

Jay finished his steak and looked at the others. "So. It looks as if there are a few fans here already," he said with a smile. "And we're not going to avoid them by hurrying. So I vote we enjoy the rest of our meal, then go out the front way, and be prepared for a bit of a crush on the way to the car. I don't want to creep out through the kitchens. What do you think?"

"Fine!" said Ben in a relaxed voice. "Who wants pudding?"

Everyone else was happy with the suggestion. Ellie thought it sounded great! Going out of the restaurant like a film star would be fun, but Piano was looking distinctly uneasy. "I don't like crowds," she said in a small voice. "Matt, why can't we go out the back?" She took hold of his arm and gazed into his eyes. "Just you and me."

Matt looked uncomfortable. "I can't split from the boys," he told her. "And it would be mean to our fans for us to avoid them."

Jay leaned forward. "I understand if you have a problem with crowds," he said sympathetically. "But don't worry. There won't be a problem if you leave on your own. And I know the manager will let you out the back way if you don't want to use the front. Honestly."

Piano looked anxious. "But I don't *want* to leave on my own," she said. "Francesca? You're in charge."

Francesca looked harassed. "If you have a problem with crowds you certainly ought to avoid them," she said. "And the way to do that is to leave without the boys. I'd come with you, but I can't abandon Ellie. I'm responsible for you both, but I can't split myself in half." She thought for a moment. "It's not fair to drag Ellie away because of your problem," she said reasonably. "Besides, she's on an assignment. I think Jay is right. The best thing would be for you to leave quietly on your own. *Heart* will pay for a cab back to the office if you like."

Piano looked mutinous. "I might as well just get the bus home," she said. "But I'll decide what to do right before we go. I might still come with you."

"Well, good!" said Jay. "If you're sure."

Piano didn't seem at all sure, but there was a stubborn look in her eyes.

There was silence for a few seconds, and then Francesca smiled at everyone around the table. "Right then. Was Ben suggesting pudding?"

Piano didn't want pudding, but Ellie most certainly did. "Well…"

Jay offered her the menu. "I'm going to have the chocolate brownie with hot chocolate sauce and vanilla ice cream," he said.

"I'm going to have the selection of puddings," said Matt. "I've had it before. You get a little bit of everything on a huge plate. It's brilliant!"

"Pig!" said Ben. He hesitated. "I'll have the same."

Ellie laughed. "I'll have the fresh fruits with dipping chocolate," she said, wanting to try something she'd never had before. "It sounds delicious."

"And I'll have chocolate brownie like Jay," said Al with a smile to the waitress, who was hovering again. "Thanks."

"Can you do me some fruit like Ellie but without the dipping chocolate?" said Francesca. The waitress nodded.

The puddings certainly were delicious. Ellie had trouble identifying all of the many fruits she was given with her pot of dipping chocolate, but she loved every one, and the chocolate was heavenly. Al insisted that she try his brownie, and that was wonderful too. Then Ben and Matt decided that everyone ought to taste all their puddings too, and vote for the best. Even Francesca agreed to join in, and soon everyone was tasting and giving their opinions.

At last, the plates were all more or less empty, and Ellie sat back feeling very full and rather sticky. It had been a wonderful meal, but she really did need to go and wash her hands before they left. She pushed back her chair and made for the door.

"Don't be long," said Jay. "Our car will be here in a few minutes."

"I won't," she assured him.

She followed the signs to the ladies' and went in. It was a very grand room, with small individual linen towels provided in neat piles by the sinks. She took one to dry her hands, hoping she was doing the right thing. Fortunately, a few had already been used, so she could see that she was expected to drop hers afterwards into a large basket for laundering. She paused to take a tissue for her pocket and a drop of fantastic smelling lotion for her hands and then hurried back to the grill room, her wonderful Pirate shoes clicking on the polished marble floor.

Francesca was already signing for the meal, and everyone else was getting up from the table.

"The car is here," said Al. "And apparently there is a bit of a crush outside. Make sure you stick with us. We don't want to get separated."

"Hang on," said Jay, grabbing a menu and taking a pen out of his pocket. He quickly signed it and passed it to Matt. "For the waitress," he said to Ellie. "She's been really good, not saying anything to us. I know she's probably been told not to, but I could see how it was killing her!"

Al and Ben signed the menu too, then Jay took it over to where the waitress was standing, near the kitchen door. Ellie watched as he gave it to her, said a few words, smiled and then gave her a quick kiss on her cheek. He really was a great ambassador for the band. Ellie could see that a few moments of generosity from him had cost him little, but it would make sure that all the waitress's friends, and everyone in the restaurant would know what lovely people the members of Zone One were. And Ellie was sure that his act had been genuinely thoughtful – she could tell that Jay had been really grateful that the waitress had overcome her natural desire to accost them, and given them the time to enjoy their meal in peace. That was another point for Ellie's article.

As they crossed the marble floor and approached the front door, one of the restaurant employees joined them. "If you could just stay back a moment," he suggested. "I'll make sure the situation is under control."

Piano, who had been coming with them, turned very pale.

"Are you all right?" said Francesca.

Piano looked regretfully at the boys and then backed away. "I think I'll just..." She hastened back towards the waitress and started talking urgently to her.

Francesca looked relieved. "I'm sure that's the right decision," she said crisply. "Now, Ellie. Are you all right, or do you want us to join Piano?"

"No way!" said Ellie with such certainty that the boys and Francesca laughed.

"Come on then," said Jay, as the restaurant employee gave him a nod. "Let's go!"

Ellie felt Jay's hand in the small of her back, and suddenly she and Francesca were walking down the short flight of steps onto the pavement outside. The restaurant must have been very used to celebrities. They had rigged up rope barriers on the pavement, making a passageway through the crowd from the steps to the car. To begin with, no one took much notice of Ellie and Francesca, but when the crowd realized they were making for the car, things changed.

"They're with the boys!" someone shouted, and then it seemed as if suddenly hundreds of people were pointing their phones at Ellie and Francesca, taking numerous pictures and staring at them. Ellie wanted to stop, and talk to some of the fans – it would be good research for her article – but Francesca kept her moving. Then the girls were forgotten as everyone surged forward to catch a glimpse of the famous singers. The rope barriers were straining and the passageway to the car seemed to be getting narrower, but the back door of the car was standing wide open, with the driver there, ready to make sure they got safely in. Then Al was by Ellie's side. He put his arm round her shoulders to steady her as the crowd surged, clamouring, towards them. "It's a very friendly crowd," he said to her with a smile as the flash from a camera went off in their faces. "We're going to sign some autographs for a few minutes. Okay?"

"Of course!" said Ellie happily. "You go ahead."

Ellie was totally loving the situation! Although none of it was for her, she was lapping up the second-hand experience of being famous.

Ellie was just about to join Francesca in the car when several more camera flashlights went off in her face. A girl waved a piece of paper at her. "Are you Matt's sister?" Someone had read a lot about the band!

"No," said Ellie. "I'm..." It was far too noisy, and too complicated to explain what she was doing here. "I'm a friend," she said at last.

The girl waved her paper again. "Can you

sign it anyway?" she said. Then she waved it even harder. "Ben! Ben! Over here!"

Ben was at Ellie's shoulder now. He took the paper and signed it with a flourish, then handed it to Ellie. He seemed highly amused. "Your turn."

"You really don't want mine," said Ellie, trying to be reasonable, and give the paper back to the girl. But it was no good. The girl refused to take it until Ellie had signed, so she did, feeling a bit of a fraud as well as secretly thrilled.

Refusing all other requests from people who obviously thought she must be famous just because she was there, Ellie half-reluctantly climbed into the car and joined Francesca.

"Well!" she said, beaming all over her face. "How amazing is this?" Ellie felt rather breathless from the crush, and was sure she must look flushed, but Francesca looked as elegant as usual.

"I'm glad you're enjoying yourself," said Francesca with a smile.

"It's quite an experience!" said Ellie, gazing out at all the people, and half-wishing she was still out there with them.

A couple of minutes later the boys all tumbled into the car, full of high spirits, and the driver slammed the door. There were a couple of police officers there now and, as the driver jumped in, they cleared a space so the car could power safely away. Everyone was thrown back in their seats by the acceleration, which made Ellie want to giggle.

"Wow!" said Ben, grinning widely at Ellie and giving her a nudge with his elbow. "We're in the presence of a mega-famous superstar."

"What do you mean?" asked Jay.

Ben explained about Ellie signing the piece of paper and everyone laughed. Ellie laughed too. It *was* funny.

"Are we going back to the office?" Ellie said to Francesca.

"Well, I am," said Francesca. "I still have work to do. But you can go straight home if you like."

"Where do you live?" said Jay.

Ellie told him and he smiled. "No worries. That's not too far from the studio where we're going next." He looked at his watch. "We have to be in the studio in an hour. That gives us plenty of time to drop Francesca off and take you home as well."

"Well, if you're sure."

After a few more minutes the car drew up outside the *Heart* office building and Francesca got out.

"Thanks for the meal," chorused the boys.

"Thanks for the lift back," said Francesca. "I'll see you tomorrow, Ellie."

"Absolutely!" said Ellie.

"So how did it happen that you work at

Heart?" asked Al as the car pulled away. "You were going to tell me, but with one thing and another…"

Ellie found herself telling them all about her determination to follow in her father's footsteps and become a famous journalist. She told them how her Uncle Patrick had first got her the work placement, how scary Angel could be, how exacting Francesca was, and how unfriendly Piano had been from the very first moment. "But to be fair to Angel, it was her who invited me back after the placement was finished, and when she has time, Francesca teaches me stuff brilliantly," said Ellie. "It's only Piano I really have problems with, and I can usually deal with her okay."

"You must have impressed Angel during your work experience to be invited back. Whatever did you do?"

Ellie explained about the person who had been secretly trying to sabotage the magazine, and about how she'd helped identify her. "But really I think Angel just saw that using a junior reporter like me every now and then would appeal to the readers," she said modestly.

She sat back after she'd finished her story, luxuriating in being with the band members, especially Al. They were all totally fanciable, but Al, who had always been her favourite before she'd met them, was still her favourite now. And he seemed to like her too. Ellie knew that she had to be sensible. They were all just being kind and friendly to her, rather like four big brothers, but she couldn't help totally falling for Al. He was her idea of boy heaven.

Jay got a couple of envelopes out of the side pocket of the car and gave them to Ellie. "One for you and one for a friend," he said. "It's just a poster, and some other promo stuff. If you want it, that is?"

"Oh, yes please!" she said. "I'll give one to my friend Hannah. She totally loves your music. In fact..." If she didn't do it now she never would. "I've got our copies of your first CD with me." She blushed as she pulled them out of her bag.

"We'll be delighted to sign them," said Al.

He took the CDs from her and his hand touched hers. Ellie felt as if an electric shock had run up her arm.

"Hope you like our latest album," he said, smiling at her. "There's an advance copy in the envelope. We'll sign that too if you like."

"Yes please," said Ellie. "Thank you!" Once they had all signed, she looked at the titles of the songs on the new album. "Which one is your favourite?" she asked Al shyly.

Al leaned over and pointed at one halfway down the list. She could feel his warm breath on her neck. "That one."

"Only because you get to sing a solo," teased Ben.

"You're only jealous," Al teased back.

Then Matt and Jay started singing and the other two joined in. It was "Happy You", the one Al had said was his favourite. When it came to the solo, Ben sang with him for a couple of lines, teasingly overdoing it, but then he stopped and let his fellow band member have his moment.

"*Happy you,*" sang Al, "*walking along in the sunshine. Happy me, cos the person beside me so happy is you.*" He took Ellie's hand, and sang the song for her, looking into her eyes as he did so. Ellie wondered if she should feel that it was corny, but it wasn't corny at all, it was simply wonderful, and she felt herself dissolve.

Before the song had ended the car stopped, and Ellie was dismayed to see that they'd arrived right outside her flat. But no one asked her to get out. They were all too involved with the song, so she stayed where she was until they'd finished.

When they were done, Al smiled into Ellie's eyes, obviously pleased with the way the song had gone. For one wild moment, she wondered if she could ask him in, but she knew he'd refuse. They were due at the recording studio, and she really shouldn't be greedy. This had been such an amazing day, with so many ups and downs. A few hours ago she had thought the day was going to end in disappointment, but now it was ending far better than she could ever have hoped. She hated to leave them, but she knew she must.

She gathered her things together, and hesitated, with her hand on the door handle. "I've had a brilliant time," she told them all as the driver got out and opened the door for her. "Thank you so much. It's been amazing. The very best!"

She got out of the car, ready to head inside, but they all scrambled out after her.

"Bye, Ellie," said Jay, giving her a hug.

They all followed suit. Al was last. "It was great to meet you," he said. "Good luck in the future. And I hope all your dreams come true." He drew her to him and kissed her gently on her cheek. One last hug and they were all getting back in the car. The door slammed and the car pulled away. They waved, and Ellie stood on the pavement outside her flat, waving back until the car had disappeared out of sight. She put her hand to her cheek. Never, not ever, *ever*, would she wash that bit of her face. Not even if she lived to be a hundred!

Afterwards

As soon as Ellie's mum, Georgia, got home, Ellie abandoned the first draft of the article she was writing for Angel about the boys, and told her all about the day – though she saved the bit about the kiss from Al for Hannah.

"Goodness me, Ellie," said Georgia. "You do get yourself in crazy situations. What a day!"

Ellie pulled the CD and the promo things out of the envelope to show her mum.

"Put it on," said Georgia. "We can listen while we make the tea."

"Okay."

When it came to "Happy You", Ellie stopped what she was doing and simply listened, reliving every moment of the song. Her mum watched her.

"My," said Georgia when the song came to an end. "You have got it bad. They must have been quite something!"

"Yes," said Ellie dreamily. "He was."

The Easter holidays had been wonderful and one of the best things was that her aticle would appear in the next issue of *Heart*. She couldn't wait! But then, on the last day, a letter came for her. Sophie had her new post trolley, and was delivering all the office post. She put Ellie's letter on her desk with a flourish and Ellie picked it up in surprise.

"What's this?"

Sophie laughed. "A letter, you idiot. What do you think it is?"

"But I never get letters here," said Ellie. "I don't *often* get letters at home. Who could it be from?"

"Only one way to find out!" said Sophie with a laugh as she went to put the rest of the post on Piano's desk.

Ellie looked at the letter. The address was typewritten, and franked, and Ellie could make nothing of the postmark. She opened it up and two tickets fell out. To her astonishment, they were tickets for the opening gig of the upcoming Zone One tour. The seats seemed to be right at the front too, judging by the seat numbers.

"What have you got there?" It was Piano. Usually she affected total disinterest in whatever Ellie was doing, but she must have caught sight of the tickets.

"Um…tickets for the Zone One gig, later this year," said Ellie. She looked in the envelope and found a handwritten note from Al.

Hope you and Hannah can use these. It was great to meet you. Keep at the journalism. I'm sure you'll be as famous as us one day. You've

already got the hang of signing autographs!
Love, Al xxx

Ellie became aware that Piano was still talking to her. "I expect my letter is in with the rest of the post." Piano hesitated, and looked down her nose at Ellie. "But I wouldn't go to the first gig if you paid me. It's far better to wait and go later on, once they've got into it. They'll be really shaky on the first gig." She stalked off, swaying slightly on her high heels.

You liar! thought Ellie with a small smile to herself. *Of course you'd go if you had tickets, but you're a bit worried they haven't sent you any!*

Ellie couldn't wait to tell Hannah about the tickets. She pulled her phone out of her bag and texted her straight away, even though she knew that Angel didn't approve of private texts being sent during office hours. Almost straight away a text came back.

You are my best friend ever!!! it said. *I can't*

wait! And tickets at the very front? Wow wowie
wow! I wonder if they'll sing Happy You?

Ellie put the tickets and note back in the
envelope and hugged it to herself. If the tickets
really *were* in the front row, and if they *did* sing
"Happy You", it would take her right back to
that amazing day at the beginning of the
holiday. And although Ellie *had* washed her
cheek where he'd kissed it, she knew she'd
never forget Al from Zone One, singing the
song just for her.

For wannabe journalist, Ellie, doing work experience at her fave teen magazine is a dream come true. Check out the other titles in this stylish series:

My life behind the scenes at...

Heart
Magazine

A dream come true

Pop

Celebrity

Gossip

ISBN: 9781409520207

Cindy Jefferies

A dream come true

Ellie's got a jealous rival who's determined to turn her dream job into a nightmare...

My life behind the scenes at...

Heart Magazine

Search for a star

Cindy Jefferies

ISBN: 9781409520221

Search for a star

Can the Editor's pampered pooch help Ellie track
down the star she'd love to interview?

Best friends rock!

Ellie's fallen out with her best friend and an
interview with the son of a rock star is a disaster.
Will things ever go right this summer?

Cindy Jefferies is also the author
of the fabulous

Fame School

Look out for:

Reach for the Stars   9780746061176
Chloe loves to sing and dreams of becoming a
pop star. But will she win a place at Fame School?

Rising Star   9780746061183
Chloe is desperate to perform in the Rising Stars
concert, but will her voice be strong enough?

Secret Ambition   9780746061206
Model twins Pop 'n' Lolly have always done everything
together. But one of them has a secret ambition.

Rivals!   9780746061190
Danny's drumming talents are in demand, but his
jealous rival is out to cause trouble.

Tara's Triumph   9780746068359
Tara wants to produce a charity CD with her friends, but
will it be more trouble than she bargained for?

Lucky Break
9780746068366

Marmalade is always showing off, but when a new boy starts looking up to him, he takes things a step too far.

Solo Star
9780746073032

Chloe is thrilled to be picked for the Rising Stars concert, but can she learn how to sing with a band?

Christmas Stars
9780746077429

Can Chloe and her friends impress their favourite teacher with a surprise Christmas concert performance?

Pop Diva
9780746073049

Pop 'n' Lolly have won a recording contract, but will Pop work hard enough to make their single a success?

Battle of the Bands
9780746078839

Does Chloe's band still stand a chance of winning the International Battle of the Bands after disaster strikes?

Star Maker
9780746097151

Tara's band is set to play a massive charity gig on TV! But will it all go wrong when their drummer falls ill?

Dancing Star
9780746097168

Marmalade has been picked to dance in a pop video, but will his new-found creative flair impress his friends?

Summer Spectacular
9781409505129

School's out for summer, but the Fame School friends put on a party to remember…

Trick or Treat
9781409509769

There are some spooky things going on. Is someone playing tricks or is Fame School haunted?

Cindy Jefferies' varied career has included being a Venetian-mask maker and a video DJ. She started out training to be a teacher, but soon left, and went to live in a caravan on the west coast of Scotland instead. She has traded in junk antiques, worked in shops and even tried telesales. But in her heart she has always been a writer, ever since she first learned to read.

Cindy lives between town and country – with deer and foxes one side of her garden, and shops and buskers a few minutes' walk away from the other. Her ideas come from what she hears and sees around her, and from deep inside her head.

To find out more about Cindy Jefferies, visit her website: www.cindyjefferies.co.uk

Grace and glamour, danger and determination – check out
Skate School *by Kay Woodward*

Ice Princess

Frankie lives for ice-skating and has her heart set on becoming a star. It's a dream come true when she's whisked off to Skate School to train for Olympic glory.

ISBN 9780746099254

On Thin Ice

Frankie's thrilled when she's chosen to skate with Paul. But Paul doesn't want to share the spotlight with anyone. It's a problem as they're meant to be competing in Perfect Pairs. Together.

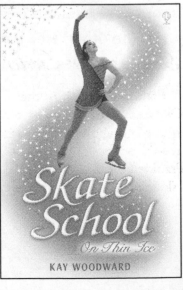

ISBN 9780746099261

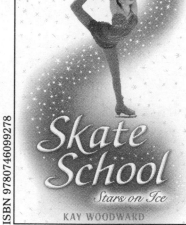

Stars on Ice

Frankie's got her sights set on winning at the World Championships. She's also falling for the gorgeous Dylan. But romance is forbidden at Skate School. Will their secret skating get found out?

ISBN 9780746099278

Going for Gold

Frankie's made it to the Olympics and she's going for gold. But one of her rivals will stop at nothing to win. Can Frankie keep a cool head and skate to perfection when it matters most?

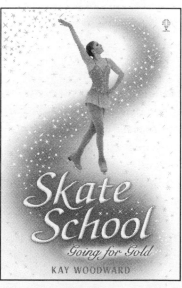

ISBN 9780746099285

For more stylish reads
check out
www.fiction.usborne.com